"We're in a c▮▮▮▮▮

The woman struggled to sit up▮▮▮▮▮▮▮
and pointed out the spiderwebbed front windshield
down the road from where they had fled.

"I only want to see my little girl again. Please, you
have to help me see her again."

Her voice was too raw with emotion for it to be a
lie, and Bolan couldn't help but respond with the
same honesty.

"I will, I promise you, I will help you. But you have
to help, you have to fight."

"Here they come!" she cried.

The Executioner whipped his head around and
saw headlights appear out of the darkness, bearing
down on them with deadly speed. He snarled and
continued driving. The vehicle was shaking apart
from the brutal beating it was taking on the rough
road. The woman fought her way into a sitting
position and snapped her seat belt into place as
Bolan pushed the gas pedal to the floor.

Then the grenades began to rain down.

MACK BOLAN ®
The Executioner

The Executioner®
Don Pendleton's
DESPERATE PASSAGE

A GOLD EAGLE BOOK FROM
W⦾RLDWIDE®

TORONTO • NEW YORK • LONDON
AMSTERDAM • PARIS • SYDNEY • HAMBURG
STOCKHOLM • ATHENS • TOKYO • MILAN
MADRID • WARSAW • BUDAPEST • AUCKLAND

First edition October 2008

ISBN-13: 978-0-373-64359-2
ISBN-10:   0-373-64359-4

Special thanks and acknowledgment to
Nathan Meyer for his contribution to this work.

DESPERATE PASSAGE

Between two groups that want to make inconsistent kinds of worlds, I see no remedy except force.

—Oliver Wendell Holmes, Jr.
1841–1935

When there is no option but force, I will be that force.

—Mack Bolan

THE
MACK BOLAN

LEGEND

Nothing less than a war could have fashioned the destiny of the man called Mack Bolan. Bolan earned the Executioner title in the jungle hell of Vietnam.

But this soldier also wore another name—Sergeant Mercy. He was so tagged because of the compassion he showed to wounded comrades-in-arms and Vietnamese civilians.

Mack Bolan's second tour of duty ended prematurely when he was given emergency leave to return home and bury his family, victims of the Mob. Then he declared a one-man war against the Mafia.

He confronted the Families head-on from coast to coast, and soon a hope of victory began to appear. But Bolan had broken society's every rule. That same society started gunning for this elusive warrior—to no avail.

So Bolan was offered amnesty to work within the system against terrorism. This time, as an employee of Uncle Sam, Bolan became Colonel John Phoenix. With a command center at Stony Man Farm in Virginia, he and his new allies—Able Team and Phoenix Force—waged relentless war on a new adversary: the KGB.

But when his one true love, April Rose, died at the hands of the Soviet terror machine, Bolan severed all ties with Establishment authority.

Now, after a lengthy lone-wolf struggle and much soul-searching, the Executioner has agreed to enter an "arm's-length" alliance with his government once more, reserving the right to pursue personal missions in his Everlasting War.

1

Mack Bolan stood on the runway at Diego Garcia.

The thirty-seven-mile long atoll sat in the Indian Ocean just over one thousand miles south of the southern coast of India. It formed a sort of geographical aircraft carrier for U.S. military forces, with a runway long enough to accommodate the heaviest planes in the Air Force.

Bolan closed his eyes to the warmth of the sun and turned his face toward the sea breeze coming through the lush tropical vegetation. He wore a flight suit devoid of identification and rank. It was splattered with blood.

Diego Garcia curved around a twelve-mile-long lagoon nearly five miles across. The atoll was a joint British and American venture and had become increasingly pivotal to U.S. strategic interests since its inception as a military base in 1971.

It had served as the launching pad for Marine Prepositioning Squadron Two and similar units designated as logistical support of naval and army units. It had also been rumored to be a clandestine location site in the government's controversial Extraordinary Rendition program for terror detainees.

The base commanding officer hadn't batted an eye when presented with paperwork originating from the director of National Intelligence, instructing him to give the unidentified man before him every operational courtesy while maintaining complete indifference as to his purpose.

Bolan put a foot on the heavy pack at his feet. A slim wireless ear jack was set into his right ear, and it chirped. Bolan pressed a finger to the device.

"Go ahead," he said quietly, the sensitive microphone picking up his speech vibrations through the hard, prominent angle of his cheekbone.

"We're coming in now," Jack Grimaldi said.

"Copy, Jack," Bolan replied.

He turned his head toward the horizon and was able to immediately pick out the quickly growing shape of the C-12 Huron, the military version of the twin-engine Beechcraft King Air model airplane.

Grimaldi touched the aircraft down gently and braked along the runway, following instructions from military air traffic controllers. Bolan reached down and shouldered the heavy pack at his feet. An M-4 carbine was strapped to the outside. While waiting, he had spent some time disassembling and cleaning the weapon.

As Grimaldi taxied the plane toward him, the Execu-

tioner turned and threw a salute at the two officers of
the British Indian Ocean Territory Police who had
served as his escorts. They waved back as the rear door
of the Huron was opened by Charlie Mott and Bolan
headed for the lowered stairs.

Bolan nodded to Mott as he ducked inside the
stripped-down cabin of the plane and threw his heavy
bag on a seat.

"How'd Somalia go?" Mott asked. He buttoned up
the aircraft hatch.

"About as well as could be expected," Bolan allowed.
"Where did you guys fly out of?"

"SOCOM base in Djibouti. Were you aware the
French Foreign Legion travels with its own brothel?"
Mott asked.

"I had heard that," Bolan said.

"Go figure," Mott said, incredulous. "Anyway, let's
get off the ground, then we'll hook you up with what
Stony Man has cooking."

"Thanks, Charlie."

Bolan secured himself as Mott made his way back
up the center aisle to join Grimaldi in the cockpit. He
heard the engines rise as Grimaldi turned the nose of the
Huron around he looked out the window beside his seat
to watch the tarmac go sailing by.

He felt the thrust of the turboprops push him back
into his seat, and he knew Grimaldi had put the nose of
the plane in the air. He watched the serpentine twist of

Diego Garcia disappear beneath him as they made a run toward open ocean.

With grim finality Mack Bolan put the bloody horrors of Somalia behind him.

AFTER GRIMALDI HAD REACHED his cruising altitude and engaged the autopilot, he left the cockpit and opened a safe set into the front wall of the passenger compartment. He removed a laptop Bolan knew would be outfitted with encrypted sat-com upgrades and brought it over to where Bolan was seated, absently picking through a spaghetti dinner MRE he had pulled from his bag.

Grimaldi grinned as he handed over the computer. "We're on course for Jakarta. It's about two thousand miles, so it'll take a few hours, plus the in-flight refueling operation. We'll have you over the LZ on time though."

"No rest for the weary," the Executioner said.

The pilot shook his head. "No, there's always some bushfire that needs pissing on. This one is more last minute than most. Charlie and I have been in air the whole way from the Farm, refueling in flight as needed except for the touchdown in Djibouti. They want you in Indonesia *yesterday*."

"Barb wants everything yesterday. It's why she's the best."

Grimaldi nodded. "True enough. I'll leave you to it." he stood and tapped an overhead compartment. "You'll find a cooler in there of a little microbrew lager I stumbled across. Help you wash some of the Somalia taste out of your mouth. I'll radio home and tell them you're booting up."

"Thanks," Bolan said and opened up the laptop.

The videoconferencing software fired up with a smooth hum. The LEDs blinked into life, and the digital camera rapidly focused its lens. Bolan saw Barbara Price, Hal Brognola and Aaron "The Bear" Kurtzman. He knew from long experience that his own face was being projected onto the big screen TV wall mounted in the Stony Man War Room. He greeted his old friends and close comrades.

"Hey, Striker," Brognola greeted. "You feeling okay?"

"I could use a nap, but I'll get one soon enough."

"You up for a jump?" Price asked from beside Brognola.

Bolan narrowed his eyes. "Sure. What's the LZ?"

"An old landing strip in the mountains outside of Jakarta," Kurtzman said. "Used to be part of a heroin smuggling operation the DEA shut down about a decade ago with the help of the Indonesian government. Too overgrown to land a plane, but should serve just fine to parachute onto."

"From how far up?" Bolan asked.

"Well, the Indonesian government has got army patrols all through there so, Jack's going to feign engine trouble on the approach into Jakarta and dip down to five hundred feet," Kurtzman answered.

"I take it the Man didn't run this one past our *allies*?" Bolan said.

"I think I'd better let Hal start from the beginning," Kurtzman replied.

"DEA has been very busy throughout the region—Malaysia, the Philippines, Indonesia, all of the South China Sea countries, really. Attacking those operations where there's cross connection between terrorist activities and narcotic traffickers," Brognola began.

"Plenty of that in Indochina," Bolan stated. "I thought the government was part of the problem."

"Typical Third World split personality. Some elements are working with us, taking our financing and aid while smiling to our faces. Then corrupt elements of the same regime climb into bed with the bad guys. Indonesia is especially bad when it comes to piracy through the Strait of Malacca, but they have opium problems as well."

"If you click on the tab to the left of your screen," Kurtzman interrupted, "you'll see a photo."

"That's Zamira Loebis," Price informed him.

Bolan clicked on the link and looked at the unsmiling image of a middle-aged Indonesian man in a military uniform. He was very thin.

"He's a particular thorn in our side." The Stony Man mission controller continued. "He's the assistant minister of defense. We have him tied into piracy and heroin smuggling, often using Muslim extremist groups as cutouts while keeping a death squad of government commandos as personal muscle and bodyguards."

"We also have him pegged as a traitor working as a stringer for both Chinese and Vietnamese intelligence agencies," Brognola added. "He's very well connected with a lot of resources and a strong network of criminal activity funding his villa in the Swiss Alps and plantations in Kenya."

"The DEA has a crucial informant in a safehouse in Jakarta," Price said. "We've arranged a flight back to the U.S. where the man will testify about Indonesian corruption and several worldwide networks linking Jemaah Islamiyah and Abu Sayyef with ex-Taliban opium growers in Afghanistan. It's a real intelligence coup, and it's just what we need to bring more political pressure to bear on some of the countries who've been dragging their feet on antiterror measures."

Bolan knew Jemaah Islamiyah, sometimes referred to as JI, had burst onto the world stage in 2002 with the Bali car-bombing incident that had claimed the lives of over two hundred innocent people on the second anniversary of the bombing of the USS *Cole* in Yemen. The group itself had been around since the 1970s in one incarnation or another. It was closely linked to Abu Sayyef in the Philippines and al Qaeda.

"What's the catch?" the Executioner asked.

"The usual," Brognola growled. "According to our intel, our very well connected defense minister doesn't want the informant to make it to trial. A Kopassus hit team has been assembled."

Bolan knew of the special forces unit by reputation. Kopassus had earned a grim reputation for its special operations in East Timor and against rebel separatists in the Achen province as well as covert activities in Jakarta itself.

"We didn't tell the good guys in the government?" he asked.

"The Man would like to use the opportunity to send those corrupt government elements a very pointed message about spilling American blood under the guise of being our ally. The Military Liaison Element in Jakarta has the location where the hit team is held up waiting for our guys to move the witness. The Oval Office holds the opinion that if that hit team goes belly up, it might just shake some sense into those rogue elements."

"Should be doable if the intelligence on the hit team is right," Bolan said.

"It is," Price said. "I'll give you the rundown on the specifics. We don't want a hint of your arrival or identity so you'll need to go in black. That's why the night jump instead of civilian cover insertion."

"I understand," Bolan said.

"We have a stringer ready to facilitate your actions," Price continued. "Arti Sukarnoputri. She is a midlevel clerk with the interior ministry. She began working with the DEA when her brother, a Jakarta police officer, was

killed by corrupt government agents on a heroin investigation. She's what we were able to put together on short
notice, but stay sharp around her for now. I know this is
a little haphazard, Striker, but that hit squad is primed to
go and something has to be done, immediately. "

"We'll get that government witness out safely,"
Bolan promised.

Quickly Price began to run down the fine points of
the logistical factors.

Ten minutes later Bolan shut the laptop and put it
back in the cabin safe. Grimaldi gave him a thumbs-up
through the cockpit door and Bolan made his way back
to his seat. He eased himself into his seat and settled
back to fall asleep.

Outside the vast indigo waters of the Indian Ocean
sped by.

2

Bolan came awake instantly as Charlie Mott touched his shoulder.

"We're fifteen minutes out," Mott informed him. "Jack's already reported engine difficulty to the control tower. We'll dip down to five hundred feet, equalize things back here and put you out the door."

"I'll be ready," Bolan said.

Mott handed him a thick envelope. "I just counted it out of the safe. That's for the stringer once you link up. The stringer knows nothing about what you're doing, or why. She's there to provide transportation and navigate the locals."

"That's what Barb said," Bolan replied, nodding.

"You want me to help you suit up?"

Bolan shook his head. "No. I'll do it. Give me a couple minutes, and then you can double-check my hook-up before you kick me out the door."

Mott laughed, then retreated up the center aisle.

Bolan slid the envelope into his blacksuit, then pulled

his parachute from under a seat and began checking the harness and adjusting the straps for a good fit based on long experience.

He worked methodically, with diligent attention as he slid into his harness and readjusted the straps. He double-checked that his weapons were secure and pulled on a nondescript helmet that he buckled under his chin. He decided he was better off without it and took it back off again and tossed it under a seat.

He stood and manhandled his backpack toward the rear door of the plane where he started attaching his guidelines. His ears began to pop, and he knew Grimaldi was bringing the plane down toward jump altitude. At five hundred feet the drop would be over in an instant. He'd be out the door and on the ground so fast there'd be no room for miscalculation of any kind.

Mott began making his way toward Bolan. The Executioner felt the plane tilt sharply as Grimaldi began his circle over the landing zone. Bolan could see a dark mass of thick tropical foliage below the plane.

"Jack's told the tower in Jakarta he's compensating for a bad turboprop," Mott told Bolan as he checked the fittings on the parachute harness. "The weather's clear with a half moon. The old landing strip is easy to spot in the vegetation. There's about a five mile per hour wind out of the southeast."

Bolan nodded. "I'm ready when you are."

Mott moved to the door and grasped the handle.

Bolan fitted a pair of goggles into place. After two long minutes during which Bolan could see the ground growing closer through the plane's windows, Grimaldi killed the lights in the rear compartment and Mott jerked the door open.

Bolan felt the pull of the open door. He saw the nude scar of the old, overgrown airfield and orientated himself toward it. The sound of the plane's engines was deafening. He shuffled forward, and Mott slapped him on the back as he went through the doorway into space.

The slipstream took him and he was buffeted away from the cruising aircraft. He pulled his rip cord almost immediately. The chute unfurled behind him then popped and his free fall was over. He plummeted toward the earth, the parachute hardly seeming to slow his rate of descent. His eyes quickly adjusted to the low light, and treetops sped toward him beneath his dangling boots.

He twisted hard and let the backpack dangle. The pack struck the ground and he overshot it. He hit with both feet and felt the impact slam all the way up his body, immediately rolling and absorbing the landing.

Bolan quickly popped up and stripped away the harness connecting him to the parachute. He tore off his goggles and drew his Beretta machine pistol from its sling under his arm. He turned in a slow circle, looking for danger. Seeing nothing, he quickly began gathering in his parachute and shouldering his bag.

He marked the position of the low hanging, half

moon and headed to the east of the abandoned airfield. The old landing strip was made of hard-packed dirt dotted with patches of shrubs and jungle grass. Just on the edge of the field the Indonesian jungle encroached aggressively. At the end of the landing strip was an ancient, dilapidated Quonset hut hangar where his stringer had been told to meet him.

In order to increase operational security the stringer hadn't been informed of how Bolan was making his approach to the meet, only the location. Skirting the tree line, Bolan made his approach toward the abandoned structure.

He slipped into the shadows of the trees and bushes before putting away the Beretta and concealing his parachute gear in the undergrowth. He took his M-4 carbine from his pack when he was finished.

A rickety chain-link fence encircled the hangar, and the windows set into the structure were all broken. Nothing moved.

As Bolan drew closer to the building, his instincts alerted him to trouble. He then saw the earth in front of the fence gate was freshly turned up in semicircular patches, revealing darker earth and, once he was close enough, tire treads.

Bolan adjusted the grip on his M-4 and moved out of the nominal safety of the tree line. He stopped at the fence. One of the gates hung from only a single hinge. The frame was bent near the center, and rested, old metal had been scraped clean. A medium strength steel chain hung limp from the fence links. Bolan picked it up and inspected it. The chain had been broken cleanly through on one of its individual links.

Bolan saw something in the turned up earth and bent to retrieve it. It was an old key-operated lock. A bit of the broken chain fell away as he plucked it from the mud where it lay in the middle of a wide tire track.

Bolan looked up, scanning the silent hangar.

He moved through the gate and put himself at an angle to the door, then jogged forward and put his back to the wall next to the slightly open sliding door.

He paused for a moment, listening, but heard only the silence. Steeling himself, he flipped around the corner and penetrated the dilapidated hangar, M-4 up and leading the way. He moved out of the light of the opening quickly and took up a defensive position on one knee beside the sliding door. He felt the hard cylinders of spent brass under his knee and detected the aroma of cordite.

He flicked his muzzle around the cavernous hangar and found nothing.

The meet location was deserted.

The Executioner left the building and hurried across the short stretch of yard between hangar and ramshackle fence. As he searched the environment, he saw a black pool that had been hidden in shadow. He knelt beside it and reached out his hand, his fingers coming away sticky and damp. He took in the copper-tang smell, confirming his obvious suspicions. The pool was blood, and whoever had been wounded had either made his or her escape or the body had been taken away to hide evidence.

Bolan rose and made for the shelter of the jungle.

THE EXECUTIONER his GPS unit and noted the time on his watch. He was early, as the plan had called for, giving him time to recon the area around the contingency rendezvous zone. He let his sniper's eye take in his surroundings, cataloging them with terse efficiency, discounting shadow, penetrating dark while his ears strained to catch even the slightest and most innocuous of sounds.

The stringer, Arti Sukarnoputri, had been told to meet him at a given coordinate should the initial contact not be made, but not how Bolan had made his insertion. That had been a deliberate precaution to avoid his being captured should Sukarnoputri prove duplicitous. But Bolan knew the fact that he had not been immediately ambushed was in no way a guarantee that the Indonesian stringer was legitimate.

A she watched the old logging road, his finger rested on the smooth metal curve of the M-4 carbine's trigger. Gnats, thirsty for the salty flow of his sweat, descended on him in a cloud and he could feel them batting against his face. He made no move to shoo them away.

The minute hand on his watch moved and on cue headlights appeared in the curve on the road from the north. Bolan frowned and grasped the stock of the carbine tightly. The car was moving too quickly for the road conditions.

The vehicle was unidentifiable in the deep gloom. He remained motionless as the car skidded to a stop on the dirt road precisely at the spot he had noted with GPS readings. The driver's door was thrown open and Bolan saw a slim figure hop out, leaving the engine running and breaking the protocol for the meet.

"You are a long way from home! You are a long way from home!" a feminine voice hissed in a frantic tone.

Bolan rose and was forced into making a decision. The stringer had been instructed to stop her car, kill the engine and lights before getting out and moving to the rear of the vehicle. There Bolan would approach her. Upon seeing him she was to say "You are a long way from home." His reply would be "Home is where you hang your hat."

It was simple, direct and slightly cliché in the way most tried and true methods often were. Anything other than the proper protocol and Bolan was supposed to avoid the contact. This was an extreme deviation Bolan readjusted his grip on his M-4.

Suddenly, from the direction the stringer's car had driven, a second and then a third set of headlights appeared. Bolan saw the women turn her head toward the light.

Once again she called out, and Bolan was able to hear the racing of the other two car engines as the vehicles sped toward the rendezvous site. He gritted his teeth then committed himself to his course.

"Home is where you hang your hat," he snapped and rose from the shadow of the bushes.

"Thank God!" the woman said in heavily accented English. "Hurry! Those are Laskar Jihad!"

Bolan sprang forward as the woman ducked back behind the wheel of her vehicle. Bolan snatched open the rear door and threw his pack inside before slamming the door and jumping into the front passenger seat.

He had barely touched the leather seat before his contact floored the gas pedal of the SUV. The vehicle shot forward down the rough and potted secondary road, bouncing hard and rattling Bolan's teeth. He fought his way around in the seat to look out the rear hatch window. The chase vehicles had closed a little bit of the distance.

"Laskar Jihad," he said. "They aren't supposed to be active in this area."

"Your intelligence is wrong. They entered into an operational alliance with Jemaah Islamiyah. They undertake activities in the highlands around Jakarta, drawing resources while JI conducts attack in the city. Besides, I'm almost positive Zamira Loebis is running them through bribes," the woman said.

Bolan didn't know whether to believe her. It seemed too coincidental that his contact should arrive under fire, potentially killing his own mission before it had even begun. Still, the situation on the ground in Indonesia was extremely fluid, and half-a-dozen terror groups operated in the poverty stricken country. But it would have been easier to simply ambush him.

"Pop the hatch," he ordered.

He crawled between the front two seats and into the back of the SUV, folding one of the seats down to sprawl out in the back.

"What are you doing?" The woman shrieked.

"Shut up!" Bolan snapped. "Do what I say and pop the hatch!"

The woman swore, then reached down and yanked on the plastic lever controlling the catch release. The rear hatch popped open and swung up, revealing the racing road just beyond the bumper. The two vehicles were following close behind.

Bolan was tossed to one side as the SUV dipped into a rut and bounced out on the other side. He grunted under the impact but maneuvered his M-4 into position. The hydraulic support struts caught, locking the hatch door open.

From the darkness next to the windshield of the first chase vehicle a sudden brilliant star-pattern burst erupted. Bolan heard the unmistakable sound of 9 mm rounds being burned off. The SUV lurched hard to the side as Sukarnoputri wrestled it around a corner.

Bolan used his thumb to click the fire selector switch on his carbine to the 3-round burst position. He spread his legs wide in the rear compartment to equalize his balance and dug in with his elbows to steady his weapon. The buttstock slapped into his cheek and opened a cut as the SUV drove over a jutting rock shuddering the vehicle on its frame.

Bolan ignored the stinging wound and crammed the stock back into the pocket of his shoulder. The headlights of the first vehicle appeared around the tree-choked turn of the road, and Bolan caught a brief flash of a human figure hanging outside the passenger window of a battered white truck.

Bolan squeezed his trigger and saw the left headlight on the truck wink out as one of the 5.56 mm rounds struck home.

The submachine gunner on the truck's passenger side returned fire, burst for burst, but the effect of speed and road conditions on the two men's aim made the duel nearly futile for several exchanges.

The Executioner rode out another jarring pothole and adjusted his fire. Suddenly the SUV hit a patch of gravel. He felt the rocking lurches of the road give way to an almost even vibration as the SUV slide across the gravel, and he squeezed the trigger on his M-4.

He put two 3-round bursts into the front windshield of the pickup, shattering it. The pickup swerved hard to the right and the front tire rolled up an embankment. It rolled onto its side as it half climbed the embankment, then slammed into the gnarled and twisted trunk of a squat jungle tree. The hood crumpled under the impact, then the truck flipped. It struck the broken road hard, the cab smashing flat with a crunch followed immediately by the thunderclap of metal on metal as the second chase vehicle slammed into the first. The overturned truck spun away from the contact like a child's top while the second vehicle lost control and careened off into the heavy underbrush beside the road.

Bolan scrambled up and grabbed hold of the open rear hatch from the inside and yanked it closed.

"You killed them all!" Sukarnoputri shouted as Bolan shoved himself back into the front seat.

"I doubt it," Bolan muttered. "And stop shouting."

"Whatever you say!"

"How did you know that was Laskar Jihad?" Bolan asked, buckling his seat belt. He placed his still smoking M-4 carbine muzzle down between his legs.

"I know because I know. They tried to stop me at a roadblock where this access road starts off the main regional highway. Your people gave me very good car. I drove into the ditch and around them, no slowing down. But they caught up with me at the hangar. I got away."

"Good job," Bolan said.

"I want more money. This was a stupid place to pick you up."

"I'm not the company accountant. And I needed to get to Jakarta in a hurry."

"Why? What do you have to do?"

"You're not getting paid to ask questions," Bolan pointed out. "And slow down. No one's chasing us anymore. You're going to shake my teeth out of my head if you don't wreck us first."

"First I do good driving then you're worried I'll wreck you?"

Bolan turned to look at his driver. She was slim and pretty with raven hair. When she took her eyes off the road to meet his he saw a calculating intelligence.

Bolan turned his attention toward the road. A thick wall of tropical forest formed a shadowy corridor along the logging road. Vines, branches and rotted logs had fallen across the single lane, forcing Sukarnoputri to swerve the vehicle around the obstacles while navigating potholes, rain-wash trenches and protruding rocks.

"Where are we going?" he asked.

"Offroad, back down to the regional highway, then the road into Jakarta. Forty-five minutes, maybe one hour."

"Patrols? Roadblocks? More Laskar gunmen?" Bolan asked.

"Possible. There are Indonesian marines in the area to combat Laskar's influence. Sometimes it works, sometimes not."

They rounded the corner fast and Sukarnoputri screamed. Headlights filled the windshield as another car raced up the narrow road toward them. Sukarnoputri yanked the wheel hard to one side, swerving to avoid the onrushing vehicle. The SUV lurched to the left, and there was a horrendous screech as the two vehicles skidded off each other. A shower of sparks formed a rooster tail in the driver's window, and Bolan had an impression of a battered jeep filled with figures.

Immediately behind the first vehicle was a second, and Bolan caught a glimpse of a third set of headlights beyond. Then the front of the SUV bucked up hard and came down, leaving the windshield filled with the leaves and branches of jungle foliage.

Sukarnoputri tried to turn the SUV back out of the jungle, but suddenly the massive trunk of a tree appeared in front of the out of control SUV. Bolan threw his arms up instinctively.

The impact was followed by the violent reversal of momentum. As the hood crumpled and the fender was bent inward, Bolan was thrown hard against his seat belt. He felt something smack his face, then heard the air bags deploying.

He was blinded by the emergency cushion and could see nothing of what was happening but felt the car begin to roll. His world suddenly inverted, and he was thrown against his door. Then just as suddenly he slid up in his restraint to bang his head on the roof as the SUV completed its roll and landed on its blown-out tires. The air bags settled, quickly deflated and Bolan sprang into action.

"Are you all right?" he asked.

He snapped the release on his seat belt and reached

for his door handle, but the door refused to budge. There was no answer from Sukarnoputri.

"Are you all right!" Bolan repeated, shouting.

"Yes, I'm fine," she said.

The Executioner threw his shoulder against the inside of the passenger door.

"Can you get out?" he asked.

"No, my door is jammed!" Sukarnoputri's voice sounded panicky.

Bolan leaned back and kicked. With a screech the stubborn door finally opened. Bolan snatched his M-4 and scrambled out.

"Come on!" he snapped.

He looked over the caved in hood and saw a short convoy of three vehicles stopped in the middle of the logging road on the other side of the thick brush from his wreck.

Two Indonesian men dressed in grungy civilian clothes and packing AKM assault rifles appeared. Bolan moved toward the rear of his vehicle as one of the men raised his assault rifle to fire. The Executioner drew a snap-bead and put the man down.

Bullets struck the ruined SUV, and Bolan sensed Sukarnoputri crawling out of the wreck behind him. He pivoted his barrel across the collapsed roof and fired a second time, putting the other man down as well.

Angry shouts came from the road and weapons up and down the length of the convoy erupted into action. A hailstorm of lead cut through the jungle, ripping the flora apart, shredding bark and leaves and riddling the SUV.

Pinned down, Bolan struggled to act.

3

The Executioner threw himself over the screaming woman.

"Crawl for that tree!" he ordered.

Twelve yards ahead of them an old jungle giant had been battered down in some monsoon gale years before. Its trunk would form a bulwark against the withering gunfire tearing up the topography around them.

He shifted his weight off her body and immediately she started scrambling forward, her belly tightly to the ground and her head down. Bolan let her crawl a body length ahead of him, then began to follow.

Sukarnoputri reached the log and made to slither over it but another burst tore splinters of wood from the dead tree and she froze.

Bolan charged forward, coming up to his hands and knees, and rammed his shoulder into her, sending her tumbling over the top. He landed atop her in a tangle of limbs. She whimpered at the treatment, but he ignored her protests and scrambled into position.

"Stay down!" he barked.

He levered his rifle barrel over the edge of the tree trunk and tore loose with a long burst of answering fire. He then rolled took a position at the end of the log where a tangled mess of old roots had been torn from the earth. He used the broken cover to quickly survey the scene.

The militia gunmen from the convoy had advanced and fallen against the road bank, using it like a berm to gain cover as they fired at their adversaries. On the left side two of the braver men had begun to creep forward under the covering fire of their teammates.

Bolan swung his carbine, spraying the wreck of the SUV. Three times he poured tight bursts into the vehicle until he managed to ignite the gas tank. The already ruined vehicle exploded into flame. Black smoke rolled off the bonfire of gas, rubber and oil. It began to choke the thick forest.

He rolled around and crawled across the ground next to the cowering Sukarnoputri. Bolan realized that necessity had put him in the company of a person completely unsuited for the situation.

"We have to move," he urged the frightened woman.

She nodded, her face streaked with tears, and Bolan was able to coax and into a crawl. He pushed her forward to speed their flight into the jungle. As he turned to cover their retreat, he saw a gunman race forward, weapon at the ready. The man's eyes squinted hard against the choking smoke, and Bolan used the advantage to put a single 5.56 mm round through his throat.

The man tumbled forward and sprawled on the ground. A second gunman leaped over the body, weapon chattering in his fists as he fired from the hip. Bolan triggered a 3-round burst that put the man down two steps from the corpse of his militia brother.

"Move!" Bolan urged.

Sukarnoputri lurched to her feet and stumbled behind the cover of a thick tree, swatting away low-hanging branches as Bolan burned off the rest of his magazine in covering fire.

The bolt on his M-4 locked open as he fired his last round, and he dumped the empty magazine as he turned and sprinted for cover. More gun-fire answered his, and bullets tore through the jungle all round him.

Bolan slid around the cover of a tree and slammed a fresh magazine home. He went to one knee and twisted around the trunk of the tree. He saw figures moving in the smoke and foliage and triggered snap bursts in their direction without striking a target. He heard an all-to-familiar shrieking sound and instinctively ducked behind the tree.

A second later the 84 mm warhead of a RPG-7 struck off to his left and exploded with savage, devastating force. Bolan felt the shock waves roll over him even through the sturdy protection of the massive tree trunk.

Shrapnel burst through the jungle and Bolan heard Sukarnoputri scream.

He rose and whirled, his ears still ringing from the explosion, and sprinted away from the battle. He stormed through the undergrowth searching. He saw the huddled woman on the ground and went to her.

He rolled her over and saw her blouse was splattered with blood and a long gash had opened across her forehead, turning her beautiful face into a mask of blood. Her breathing was rapid and shallow and her eyes flickered beneath her lids. She moaned in pain as Bolan lifted her and threw her over his shoulder in a fireman's carry.

He rose, lifting her slight form easily, and began to run.

Sukarnoputri's blood poured over him in a hot, sticky rush. His shirt clung to his skin as if glued there, and each bouncing step he took forced another agonized moan from the woman. Behind him gunshots rang out but the bullets flew wider and wider as the Executioner ducked around and through trees, heavy brush and bamboo stands.

He knew from the reconnaissance maps he had looked over prior to his jump that a Malwi river tributary down out of the mountains near his location. He was unsure how far they had driven in their chaotic ride, but he estimated the bridge for the river should be no more than a few miles from their present position.

He began to make his way back toward the road.

Roots and vines tugged at his feet, threatening to trip him up at every step. Branches slapped at his face and angry shouts chased him. He had no time to check Sukarnoputri's wounds and the slip of a woman had ceased to groan. He feared she had fallen into shock.

Bolan gritted his teeth against the strain and ran on.

He cut out of the brush minutes later and hit the road well below the initial contact site. He jogged onto the road. It was simply too hard to break a trail through the jungle with the woman on his back. For his plan to work he needed to make it to the bridge quickly and as fresh as possible.

He crossed the road and began making his way back toward the stalled convoy that had transported the men now hunting him.

When he caught sight of the convoy, he slowed his approach and took to the trees, choosing his steps carefully. The burning SUV caused light and shadow to flicker and dance across the vehicles.

Bolan paused and scanned the scene. All the vehicles, two battered Nissan Pathfinders and an even older jeep, had been left with their engines running to facilitate movement under fire. Two armed men in black and olive drab civilian clothes and headbands had been left behind to secure the vehicles.

The men stood at either end of the convoy in the middle of the road. The hectic action in the jungle kept drawing their attention away from their posts and toward the still burning hulk of Bolan's vehicle. The soldier gauged the distance and frowned. When he moved there would be no time for hesitation. Other members of the militia were calling out from the trees, close at hand.

The Executioner made his decision.

He looped the end of his rifle sling over his right shoulder. Grabbing the M-4 carbine by its pistol grip, he was able to steady his muzzle one-handed by thrusting his weapon against the pull of the sling braced against his shoulder. At this range it would be enough.

Bolan gritted his teeth and shifted the limp form of Sukarnoputri into a more comfortable position. He jogged forward out of the brush and onto the road about five yards from the tailgate of the last vehicle in the line.

He shuffled forward four steps before the sentry closest to him turned. Bolan flexed the muscles of his forearm and triggered his weapon. The M-4 bucked in his hand with the recoil of his 3-round burst. The 5.56 mm rounds caught the spinning militiaman high in the chest.

The man staggered backward at each impact before he went down. Bolan brought the M-4 to bear as the second sentry turned in alarm at the ambush. He saw the man snarl in fear and outrage as he lifted his Kalashnikov, and a burning cigarette tumbled from his mouth as he fought to bring the AKM around in time.

Bolan stopped him with a 3-round burst to the gut. The AKM tumbled to the ground and bounced before the slack corpse of the gunman pinned it to the dirt. Almost immediately a questioning cry was raised by the trailing members of the hunter-killer team deployed near the crashed vehicle.

Bolan wasted no time. Letting the M-4 dangle from its sling, he opened the door on the jeep and ducked inside. He thrust the unconscious Sukarnoputri across the seat and up against the front passenger door.

The glass in the window of the driver's door shattered as bullets slammed through it. Bolan dropped and spun, swinging the M-4 up by its pistol grip. He saw a figure at the top of the berm above the roadside.

He triggered a blast from the hip across the fifty yards and punched the man back into the underbrush. Wasting no time, he jumped behind the wheel of the jeep and slammed the door shut. Leaving his carbine across his lap, he threw the vehicle into reverse and gunned it, twisting in the seat to look out the back window.

He heard Sukarnoputri moan on the seat beside him, but he couldn't risk looking down. Still driving in reverse he navigated the primitive road as more bullets began to strike the vehicle frame and punch holes through the windows.

There was no time or space to perform a bootlegger maneuver on the narrow track, so Bolan simply drove in reverse. The windshield caught a round and spider-webbed, but the intensity of fire coming from the jungle had begun to slacken and he knew the members of the Indonesian crew were making for their own remaining vehicles.

Suddenly a screaming gunman raced into the middle of the road and took up a position in the jeep's path. Kalashnikov rounds punched through the rear windshield and burned through the space around Bolan's head. The soldier floored the gas pedal on the already erratically bouncing jeep and hurtled toward the gunman.

Green tracer fire arced through the cab of the jeep and rounds thudded into the seats. Sukarnoputri screamed at his side as the plastic screen over the gas gauge and speedometer shattered. A 7.62 mm round struck the steering wheel, and for a wild second Bolan thought it was going to come apart in his hands.

Then the speeding jeep struck the gunman. As metal made contact with flesh and pulverized it. Blood splashed into the back of the jeep, painting the seat and a battered old jerri can of gasoline.

Bolan felt the vehicle shudder as he rolled over the man. Then he was past the corpse and around a bend in the logging road.

He continued to drive in reverse, hunting for a place where the road widened sufficiently to turn the jeep around.

Driving in reverse, he was unable to use his headlights and so was unable to circumnavigate some of the more egregious ruts and potholes. The jeep was taking a brutal beating, and both he and the wounded woman were being knocked around mercilessly. She was moaning softly but when Bolan risked a glance to look at her he was surprised by how alert she appeared.

"How do you feel?" he asked. "How badly are you hurt?"

"I feel awful, dizzy and my arm and back hurt badly. But I don't think I was hurt, you know, inside," she said.

"Good, because we're in a damn tight spot."

Sukarnoputri struggled to sit up. She lifted her arm and pointed out the spiderwebbed front windshield back down the road from where they had fled.

"I only want to see my little girl again. Please you have to help me see her again," she cried.

Bolan knew her voice was too raw with emotion to be a lie, he respond with the same honesty.

"I will, I promise you. I will help you. But you have to help, you have to fight."

"Here they come!" she cried.

Bolan whipped his head around and saw headlights appear out of the darkness, bearing down on them with deadly speed.

He snarled something Sukarnoputri didn't catch and continued driving. The vehicle was shaking apart from the beating it was taking on the rough road. Sukarnoputri fought her way into a sitting position and snapped her seat belt into place. Bolan pushed the gas pedal to the floor of the jeep.

Then the grenades began to rain down.

4

Sudden flashes of light and the deafening sound of explosions hammered into the Executioner. Suddenly the steering wheel was wrenched from his grip and he felt the jeep fly into the air and tilt. He rolled, weightless, for a long moment then the vehicle crashed back to the ground and he was jarred hard against his seat harness.

He heard metal shriek in protest as the roof of the car crumpled inward and felt the frame slam into his head. He hung upside from his seat belt and his M-4 flew up from his lap and smashed his nose.

He felt the inverted jeep sliding forward, hurtling across the broken road. Dirt flew up through the shattered windshield to spray him. Fumbling with the release on his seat belt, he found it and released himself, dropping onto the crumpled hood. The jeep pitched abruptly and he was thrown against Sukarnoputri.

The vehicle slammed hard into something, and Bolan

was catapulted forward again. He buckled around the steering wheel and dropped against his seat in a heap.

His head was spinning from the blasts and the crash. He could feel a sticky mask of blood on his face and he gasped for breath. He reached for his assault rifle but couldn't find it. Pulling the Beretta clear of the sling beneath his arm, he struggled to get orientated properly.

Machine-gun fire raked the bottom of the vehicle. Bullets burned through the frame and tore the covers off the seats, stuffing exploding into the air. Bolan was clipped above the elbow and felt a hammer blow on the heel of his boot. Sukarnoputri screamed, and Bolan twisted to look as she shoved herself forward through the blown-out windshield of the car.

He waited until she was clear then followed.

"Go!" he shouted.

He reached out a hand to give her support and the jeep exploded behind him.

They were tossed through the air, everything went black.

THE ROOM WAS STARK AND BARE, devoid of furniture other than a heavy metal table shoved up against the far wall. There was a panel of lights above Bolan and a bright, hot lamp on the table pointed toward his face. A drain was set in the concrete floor at his feet. He noticed the dark stains on the metal fixtures.

His eyes slowly focused on the man standing before

him, an Indonesian in BDU fatigues devoid of rank, unit insignia or national affiliation. The man was bearded with bright, black eyes.

"Wake up sleepyhead."

Bolan looked at him.

The man leaned in close, mock concern on his face. "How do you feel? You were pretty banged up there in the accident."

Bolan said nothing.

"What is your name?" the man asked.

Bolan closed one swollen eye against the blinding glare of the table lamp. "Where's the girl?" he croaked.

The man lifted his gaze from Bolan's and nodded to another man standing nearby. Bolan had a sense of someone large moving out from around him in his limited peripheral vision.

The punch caught him flush along the jaw and rocked his head to the side. He slowly turned his head and spit blood on the floor. The thug who had hit him lifted one big fist to strike again.

The interviewer held up a hand to stop his muscle from delivering another blow.

"I ask the questions," the man said softly.

"Suli." He nodded toward the thug.

Bolan tensed, waiting for another blow but it didn't come. Instead the thickset man walked leisurely over to the metal table set against the wall. Now that Bolan's vision was clearing, he could make out items on the table. He saw various tools and implements, including pliers and knives that would be useful for torture.

He watched as Suli rummaged around on the table before picking up a clasp knife with a four-inch blade. The edge of the knife was as rusty as the drain screen on the floor at Bolan's feet.

The man turned and stalked closer to the tightly bound Bolan. The Executioner set his jaw and tensed his arms against the restraints binding his wrists behind the chair. He felt the ropes pull and shift, perhaps even give a little but only in an insignificant way. He wasn't going anywhere. He forced himself to relax as Suli stepped in front of the lead interrogator, blocking the smaller man from view.

"What is it you wanted to know?" Bolan asked. "Tell Zamira Loebis that if he wants something from me he can ask himself."

Suli looked over at the chief interrogator, but the man didn't respond.

Suli reached out and yanked Bolan's shirt by the ruined collar, then used the clasp knife to cut the garment. In an almost bored fashion Suli let the ruined shirt hang open, exposing Bolan's bruised and blood-caked torso. Behind him the interrogator looked on with glittering eyes.

"My name is Matt Cooper," Bolan said as he worked at loosening his bonds.

The interrogator came forward. "Have I impressed upon you who is in charge?"

Bolan looked away and sagged against the back of the chair as his thumb popped free of the rope coils binding his wrist. He turned his face like a defeated man and nodded dumbly. In the eyes of Indonesian he was broken, helpless.

"Good. So, Mr. Cooper, why have you invaded the sovereign lands of the Laskar Jihad, destroyed my property and killed my people?"

Bolan let his head loll on his neck. He swallowed loudly and muttered something inaudible. He had gauged the character of the two men he faced very carefully. If he were to attack Suli and reveal he'd escaped his bonds, then the interrogator would simply call for help. Suli was a thug. A sadist and a bully, but a fighter. If his boss was attacked, Suli's first instinct would be to charge forward, not to call for help.

The Executioner had established a long and bloody career exploiting the weaknesses of those who had chosen to become his enemy.

The interrogator leaned in. "What?" he snapped.

He reached out and grabbed Bolan's hair. The big American gave him a cold stare, and the sneer melted off the Indonesian's face.

Bolan slipped his arm out of the loosened ropes. His hand slapped up like the strike of a coiled snake onto the back of the interrogator's neck in a headlock.

The interrogator squawked in sudden surprise and tried to pull away. The muscles in Bolan's arm bunched as he locked the man into immobility. Bolan snapped his head brutally into the interrogator's face. He felt the man's nose pop under the jarring impact.

The interrogator's knees buckled and he dropped to the floor at Bolan's feet, dazed. Suli roared in surprised outrage at the sudden action and charged forward. Still bound to the chair Bolan could only tense in preparation.

The thickset terrorist still held the clasp knife, and it gleamed dully in the stark light of the cell as he rushed forward. Bolan made no move to slide away or dodge as Suli came down upon him.

Bolan timed his strike as precisely as he could. His free hand clutched Suli's at the wrist and he lowered his head as the Indonesian charged in.

Suli crashed into Bolan hard, like a lineman laying into a quarterback. The Executioner felt the impact flow through him. He felt the weight and momentum of Suli drive him backward, then the squeal of protest as the chains holding the chair to the floor were payed out to their length. Then the chair shattered under the force and both of the big men crashed to the floor.

Bolan felt blood hot and sticky flow across his grip and knew he had twisted Suli's knife into him, but the big man was far from dead.

Suli began to shriek in protest as the two men rolled.

Suddenly the thug was down and Bolan was up. He slammed his forehead into Suli's face twice. The Indonesian released his grip on the knife stuck in his belly, and Bolan grasped it and twisted hard.

The soldier sensed movement from behind him and whirled. He saw the interrogator pushing himself up off the floor. Bolan yanked the blade from Suli's gut and lunged. The interrogator yelped in terror and tried to dive away, but Bolan caught him in the leg just above the knee. Blood stained the man's pants as Bolan pulled the knife down with deadly force.

The man's hands went to his wounds as he fell on his back, but Bolan jerked the knife out of his reach.

"Where is the girl?" Bolan demanded.

The interrogator didn't answer or even struggle.

Bolan rose on one knee and used the blood-smeared blade of his clasp knife to cut the fragments of chair and get clear.

He stuck the knife, blade still open, in his waistband, where it was easily accessible. He realized he had minutes, possibly seconds before he was discovered. He had to seize the initiative and maintain it. He had no idea where Sukarnoputri was being kept, but time was running out. He had come to Indonesia for a reason, and he needed his contact.

It was time to get moving.

The Executioner picked up his Beretta checked the feed, the magazine and the sound suppressor. He quickly secured the rest of his equipment, getting himself ready for his run.

He crossed the blood-splattered room and headed for the heavy door. Beretta in hand, he reached out and turned the door handle slowly before gently pushing the door open a crack and looking out.

He saw a long hallway, windowless, poorly lit and grimy. From the direction Bolan was looking it ran for about thirty yards before ending at a solid door. A guard stood with a slung FN P-90 submachine gun, smoking a cigarette and knocking the ashes straight onto the floor. Bolan was sure the man was long used to hearing screams coming from the interrogation room.

Bolan moved through the doorway room in one fluid motion. He lifted the Beretta 93-R in both hands and squeezed the trigger. The pistol coughed twice and 9 mm Parabellum rounds slapped into the startled sentry. The man went down, his rifle sliding off his shoulder and his burning cigarette tumbling from limp fingers.

Bolan spun to cover the opposite end of the hall, but saw no other targets.

There were three doors in the short corridor. He quickly tried the handles on each. One was a broom closet, long disused. The other two opened into empty rooms.

There was no clue as to Sukarnoputri's whereabouts.

5

Mack Bolan was a shadow among shadows.

Crouched in a small stand of bamboo, he watched the sentry patrol using his night-night vision goggles. Around him the pungent aroma of the mangrove swamp was cloying. Above his head a sliver of yellow moon cast a soft illumination too weak to penetrate the darkness of the tropical swamp.

A swarm of gnats floated in a cloud around his face, streaked with combat cosmetics. He made no attempt to wave them away.

The sentry paced to the end of his route, looking secure and bored in his jungle redoubt. He approached Bolan's hide, an M-16 assault rifle hung muzzle down from his shoulder. The man looked like a photonegative image in the green tones of Bolan's night-vision goggles.

The Executioner remained motionless as the sentry stopped and relieved himself.

He waited as the Indonesian finished and buttoned up his fly. He could smell the cigarette smoke on the man's clothes. Beneath that was the stench of perspiration and unwashed flesh.

The man spit it as he turned away from the trees. Bolan lunged and placed his hands on either side of the man's head, twisting hard. At the same time the big American's right knee hammered into the Indonesian's back, shoving the man forward and causing him to buckle at the knees.

The sentry blacked out almost immediately. Bolan lowered his limp body to the jungle floor, rolled the limp body into the bamboo where he himself had just hidden.

The Execution pulled his silenced Beretta 93-R clear of its shoulder holster, crossed the narrow trail and melted into the undergrowth.

The site was an old mining compound. A single, unmaintained road seemed to be the only access into the area. The jungle had grown up over the shantytown where workers had once lived, but the clearing housing the mine entrance, equipment sheds, main offices and foreman barracks.

Bolan crouched at the edge of the built-up area. Triple loops of razor wire had been strung around the compound. Six buildings of rough cinder block and corrugated sheet metal were set in a U-shape around the structure housing the mine entrance and industrial elevator. An open air, thatch-roofed pagoda-style structure sat in the middle of the camp. Bolan had observed it was where the terror unit took their meals and received briefings and indoctrination. A fire burned down to coals lay untended in a rock hearth. A single sentry sat at the edge of a wooden picnic table and smoked a cigarette in the predawn gloom. In a wooden tower next to the gate leading onto the single road another sentry monitored his surroundings.

The Executioner waited patiently. He divided the camp into sectors and carefully scanned each one, making sure he didn't overlook any potential source of danger. For his entry into the hard site he would have to cross an open area directly in the tower sentry's line of sight.

Bolan prepared for the kill. Low light leaked through the cracks and windows of the compound buildings, but the hour was very late and no sound emanated from those structures. If all went according to plan, Bolan would catch the JI terror cell sleeping. He watched as the interior guard casually turned his back and directed his attention away from the front gate and gun tower.

The Executioner began his run.

Across fifty yards Bolan sighted in on the tower gunman. He braced his trigger arm against a knee and steadied the pistol with his other hand. He exhaled softly through his nostrils to slow his heartbeat. His finger found the trigger of the Beretta and immediately an Aim-Point Infrared laser, naked to the visible eye but bright as scarlet sunshine in his night-vision goggles, snaked across the distance and landed on the Indonesian terrorist.

A bright dot, clearly visible in Bolan's goggles

appeared on the tower guard's chest. With deliberate motion Bolan slowly drew the laser sight up the man's chest until it rested on the knot of the man's Adam's apple. His finger slowly took up the slack in the pistol's trigger.

The Beretta coughed.

The subsonic round jumped across the fifty yards and burrowed through the man's throat at an upward angle to core through the brain. Blood splashed out and the man sagged under the impact, dead before he had crumpled to the floor of the guard tower.

Bolan eased the tension from his trigger and pivoted the smoking muzzle, tracking for the other compound sentry. In the gap between two buildings Bolan found his target casually strolling out from under the pagoda-style roof. Bolan breathed in pungent smell of spent cordite as it mixed with the miasma of the decaying vegetation around him.

The sentry paused in his casual pacing and swore suddenly. He lifted a free hand and slapped at his neck as if just bitten by some jungle insect.

Bolan fired.

The man's head jerked to the side and he crumpled to the ground.

The Executioner raced across the ground in an easy, crouching jog his head up and scanning for trouble, the silenced muzzle of the Beretta tracking ahead of his every turn and move. He quickly navigated the obstacles of the triple strand razor wire and penetrated the compound proper.

Bolan ghosted through the compound, making his way toward his objective like a deadly wraith. He moved in a circle around the outer perimeter, carefully placing his Semtex A loaded satchel charges. His circumnavigation of the camp complete, he came up against the outer wall of the building where he believed Sukarnoputri was being held. He edged quickly around the back corner and out of sight of the rest of the compound.

At the rear of the building he stopped to consider his options. There was no back door, but four good-sized windows lined the back wall. They were open against the oppressive Indonesian heat, only thin screens separating the inside of the building from the outdoors. Bolan eased up under the first window and listened intently. He could hear the rhythmic breathing of a sleeping man.

Slowly Bolan lifted his head and peered over the lip of the window and into the building. He scanned the interior slowly picking each shape and shadow out of the cluttered mess. The building was one open room. A man slept soundly on a cot against the wall opposite Bolan's position.

Next to the door another man with a P-90 in his lap dozed in a chair. Various items of equipment, furniture and bedding were scattered around the room between the two men. Bolan turned his gaze back toward the man sleeping on the cot.

Sukarnoputri lay on the floor. Her hands and feet were bound with white plastic ties.

She looked awake but dazed, and there was no doubt that she had been violated.

Bolan narrowed his eyes, suddenly pensive as he scanned the folding card table set next to the cot. There were several items on the desktop that seemed out of place to Bolan's practiced eyes. He mentally cataloged them then proceeded with his plan.

Easing down from the window, Bolan checked his detonators. Satisfied, he began to edge his way back around the command building toward the front door. Reaching the far corner of the structure, Bolan walked openly toward the door, his pace nonchalant and his gait relaxed. He reached out as he approached the wooden steps situated in front of the entrance and pulled the screen door open.

The hinges squeaked as the door swung open, and Bolan clearly saw the bodyguard sit up in surprise at the sudden sound. The Executioner placed the muzzle of the Beretta center mass and pumped a 3-round burst into the man's chest.

Muzzle-flash briefly illuminated the shadows like lightning streaks. The man shuddered under the impact of the 9 mm Parabellum rounds and slumped from his chair to the ground. Bolan turned as the body tumbled down, anticipating the other Indonesian's response.

Sukarnoputri's eyes were wide open, and she raised herself onto her elbows to better see Bolan's dark form. The Executioner turned in her direction and started forward, bringing up the Beretta. The field commander in the rumpled bed jumped up in surprise, confusion spilling across his features even as Bolan sprang toward him.

The man let out a short, startled shriek even as the Beretta gave another harsh, deadly cough, and his forehead was cracked open like an egg. The man fell back on his bed and stared, sightless, at the roof of his hut.

Bolan went to one knee beside the bound and gagged Sukarnoputri, the Beretta held up next to the hard angles of his expressionless face. He snapped the wrist of his left hand and flicked open the blade of the clasp knife he had taken earlier from his torturer. Working quickly, he sliced through the bindings at the woman's wrists and ankles.

"Thank you," she said in a breathless rush of gratitude.

Bolan had no time to respond. The field commander had managed a scream, and though he heard no answering outcry at the moment that didn't mean it had gone unnoticed.

The big American moved quickly to the cluttered table set next to the Indonesian terror leader's bed. He found a fat wallet and an expensive cell phone, both of which he secreted in his pockets immediately. But it was the next two items that gave Bolan pause. Under the cell phone a sheaf of U.S. postage stamps commemorating the American flag were inside a clear plastic bag. Instinct motivated Bolan to take these as well. Postage was hardly an out of place desk item, but U.S. stamps in a sealed container struck the commando as odd.

Next to the sealed stamps Bolan found the strangest item of all: a slender glass vial with a tiny pump spray device on the end. He turned the vial up to catch the light.

An Indonesian terror merchant with a bottle of women's perfume on his field desk didn't add up, and Bolan took it to contemplate later.

He turned away from the table and back toward Sukarnoputri who was getting to her feet. Bolan watched the battered woman secure the Glock-17 pistol from the mattress of her tormentor.

He didn't know this woman, knew only that she had done her best to try to help him and had suffered greatly for it. He didn't need a biography to understand the simple truth of the desperate situation they shared. She was a woman, a mother, in pain and he would do his best to see her safely home.

"Let's go," he whispered.

She checked the feed on the pistol, reseated the magazine in the pistol butt and nodded. She followed Bolan as he crossed the room, stepping over the growing pool of the sentry's blood as he opened the door.

Bolan replaced his night-vision goggles and scanned the courtyard of the compound he had infiltrated. He saw no movement.

"Come on," he whispered to Sukarnoputri and he felt her draw in close behind him as he went through the door.

They crossed the compound in a crouch, weapons and heads up as Bolan led the way toward a parked vehicle he had picked out during his initial survey of the old mining camp administration site. The pickup truck was of indeterminate color in the dark. They found the doors unlocked.

Bolan slid into the driver's seat as Sukarnoputri went around to the passenger side of the vehicle. Bolan pulled a Gerber multitool from a pouch on his belt and picked quickly through the attached implements.

Finding a flathead screwdriver prong, he opened it and unceremoniously shoved the tip into the seam running along the conjoined sections of the steering wheel column. Without preamble he snapped the seam apart, heedless of the noise, and pulled out a tangled mess of wires. He used the knife blade to first slice apart the plastic tie bunching the wires together then cut apart a red and blue ignition wire.

His foot pumped the gas as he sparked the two automatic transmission wires together. The engine rumbled to life, and Bolan quickly wrapped the two stripped wires into a single braid. He then turned his attention to his remote detonators.

"Watch yourself," Bolan warned and Sukarnoputri nodded once, her face drawn and tight with the fatigue of her stress.

His strategically placed satchels, each containing of C-4 plastic explosives, began to detonate around the camp like clockwork. The explosions were deafening and their effect catastrophic.

Buildings and structures lifted from their foundations with great, sharp blasts and billowing plumes of smoke. The shattered skeletons were suddenly backlit by balls of bright yellow fire, and body parts began flying through the air. Bolan watched his charges, like dominos falling, explode in a U-shaped pattern around the sleeping compound.

He stomped down on the gas pedal. The truck's engine raced in response, then the wheels caught, spitting earth in rooster tails. The vehicle surged forward.

Wounded men stumbled out of burning buildings screaming as the truck cut through the middle of the burning camp.

Ash and flaming debris began raining down as Bolan guided the racing vehicle through the gate and into the Indonesian night.

6

As the truck punched through the gate, misty rain turned into a downpour. Bolan put the vehicle through its paces. He turned on the windshield wipers only to see they were almost instantly useless against the force of the downpour. The world took on a smeary indistinct look as the falling water formed a curtain, making it nearly impossible to see the narrow, twisting mountain road.

Bolan felt the soft give and slide of his tires as the road turned to mud. He was forced to slow his speed, and he took the opportunity to switch into four-wheel drive.

"Do you know this area?" he asked Sukarnoputri. "Do you have any idea if there are any outposts or checkpoints?"

"I don't even know who those guys were," she replied, shaking her head. "They are not Muslim extremists, they are criminals, maybe tied to pirate gangs. I don't know, but they sure aren't fundamentalists unless Zamira Loebis is paying them, which could be likely."

Bolan frowned and didn't press the woman. He hadn't fully taken her measure yet. She had performed erratically under pressure, and he was afraid that too aggressive an inquisition after the shocks she had suffered would cause her to shut down.

He let the woman sit quickly and concentrated on navigating the treacherous road. The logging track headed out of the mountains that had cradled the old mining operation. Steep drop-offs lay to one side and a sharply angled hill on the other. There wasn't a lot of room to maneuver, and Bolan focused on controlling the truck while he considered the disjointed clues he'd been given so far.

He'd encountered a civilian-dressed militia in the Indonesian hinterland. They were in charge of a prime piece of insurgent real estate and armed with high-tech, high-end machine pistols. He knew such uniformity of arms was usually seen in highly organized fighting bodies.

The field commander had American stamps and women's perfume on his desk. His contact had led a death squad straight to him, but had suffered at the hands of their captors. And, seemingly unrelated to anything around them, she had mentioned an intriguing possibility.

Pirates.

The Executioner knew Indonesian piracy was a brutal business. Twenty-five percent of all shipping commerce, and fifty percent of the oil moved by tanker, was channeled through the Strait of Malacca and the choke point of that waterway running between Malaysia and Indonesia had been like a siren call to the new breed of modern buccaneers.

The acts of piracy—always violent—ranged from haphazard amphibious smash-and-grab assaults to slightly more sophisticated kidnap for ransom operations targeting the crew to the pinnacle of seafaring criminal activities, the hijacking of not only valuable cargo, but entire vessels.

Bolan knew that thieves of any stripe would not steal anything they could not convert to cash, and the larger the haul the more sophisticated the fencing operation behind it.

Zamira Loebis had made his fortune and solidified his power by allowing the fencing of entire ship cargoes and ocean vessels. U.S. intelligence had uncovered the convergence of corrupt governments and terrorist funding pipelines.

Profits were siphoned off to fund worldwide acts of jihad as the overburdened U.S. military and intelligence agencies struggled to keep up with an agile enemy capable of morphing into new and more virulent strains at the first sign of exposure.

Bolan mulled the problem over as he drove down the mountainside. The torrential downpour increased in strength and the road grew increasingly hard to navigate. Finally he saw the blurry outline of the jungle spread out and the indistinct areas on the roadside widen up ahead. He squinted through the pouring rain and determined that the road formed a T-intersection below him and the nature of the jungle had also changed to an overarching canopy.

He felt the truck shake and rattle as it was thrust onto the rocks and dirt of a sudden rockslide.

Bolan bounced the vehicle over the obstacles and onto the rutted road. He gently tapped his brakes, felt the back end start to fishtail, then the four-wheel drive bit into the soft ground and brought the sliding vehicle under control. Up ahead a spotlight suddenly kicked on.

Sukarnoputri screamed and he stood on the brakes.

The Executioner could make out figures and shapes in the rain. He saw the familiar high, blocky outline of a Humvee. A figure was standing in front of the military vehicle, but Bolan couldn't see if the man was dressed in civilian clothing or government uniform.

The Humvee was across the muddy road with its back bumper up against the sharp incline of the hillside and its nose pointed toward the steep drop. The way was effectively barred.

For a second Bolan sat with his engine idling, illuminated in the spotlight. He rolled the window open and put the Beretta in his lap. Sukarnoputri hissed as the armed man, still an uncertain silhouette, began to approach the vehicle.

Bolan gently quieted the woman. Rain, body temperature warm, fell in through the open window and struck his exposed face and shoulder, soaking his shirt. The rainwater tasted pungent.

The gunman moved closer. He barked something in Indonesian. Bolan reached across with his right hand and worked a mechanism under the dash. He felt the frame of the truck shake as he switched from four-wheel drive to front wheel.

"What are you doing?" Sukarnoputri asked.

"Get down," Bolan answered. "I won't be able to return fire."

"What do you mean?"

The gunman stopped his approach when he heard the engine shift. He snarled something, and for the first time Bolan caught a glimpse of the man's angry face. The man lifted his M-4 carbine, taking aim.

Bolan's foot found the accelerator.

Sukarnoputri screamed as the vehicle dug in and then shot forward. The gunman hesitated, stunned at Bolan's sudden decision. He tried to simultaneously fire and to leap out of the way, failing at both.

The truck struck him and knocked him to the mud. The front tire bounced up over the man, cutting off his screams as his sternum and rib cage were crushed under the weight of the vehicle.

Bolan fought the truck off the road and up the sharply inclined hillside. He felt the front tires dig into the hard angle and begin to claw their way up. He knew that in the rain-softened earth the four-wheel drive action of the rear tires pushing in conjunction with the front tires pulling would have caused him to slide and spin.

He fought up and around the Humvee. A man jumped out of the back door of the big military vehicle, fumbling with a weapon. The back end of the truck slid out from Bolan's control and kissed the rear bumper of the Humvee hard enough to crumple metal and jar the steering wheel in Bolan's grip.

He pushed the nose of the truck around the roadblock vehicle and pointed it back down the hillside toward the logging road. Gunfire exploded from behind him. Windows shattered in the rear of the vehicle and more torrential rain lashed in.

Bolan's head snapped back hard as the front of the truck bounced out of a ditch and onto the road. Out of the dark cavern of the Humvee driver's window Bolan registered the star-flash of automatic fire in his peripheral vision. The passenger door of the truck rang with the sound of rounds striking it. Glass shattered and Sukarnoputri screamed again.

Bolan could tell this was a scream of pain rather than fear, but he couldn't take his eyes of the road for even a glance in the woman's direction. He cranked the wheel hard back around to keep from plunging over the edge and straightened the truck. More gunfire shattered the rear window, and he felt rounds whiz past his head to puncture the windshield. A bullet burned between his hands on the steering wheel and smacked into the plastic cover housing the speedometer. The radio turned on and music blared out of the speakers. In the next second the stereo face exploded in a shower of sparks and the music went silent.

The back of Bolan's seat and headrest shuddered under the impact of rounds and he winced in reflex. He punched the accelerator and slid dangerously close to the edge of the drop-off.

Bolan saw a sharp turn ahead in the road and cranked the wheel, feeling the vehicle lose traction. He turned into the slide, found his grip and gunned the truck through the turn.

For a moment the jungle and the hillside blocked him from view of the Humvee, and he was out of range of the gunfire. He tapped the brakes and risked a look over at Sukarnoputri. The woman was huddled in the passenger seat, clutching her stomach, and Bolan could see the darkness of her blood spreading out across her lap and onto the seat.

He couldn't stop to tend to her wounds, it would leave them sitting ducks for the Humvee crew that would be hard on their trail.

How this woman has suffered since she met me, Bolan thought. Her only hope lay in his ability to maneuver the shot-up truck down a twisting jungle road in the dark of a tropical deluge.

"Ball up a shirt and press it against the wound," Bolan commanded. "Try to slow the bleeding until I can do something."

Bolan's eyes found the rearview mirror, and he saw the headlights of the Humvee appear behind him. His mouth was dry as he heard Sukarnoputri moan in pain again. He sensed her struggle to comply with his directions, but he couldn't afford to take his eyes off the road.

The Humvee rushed forward behind them, its broader tires and wider wheel base giving it greater control on the treacherous surface. Bolan assumed the roadblock was intended to halt any traffic from approaching the old mining compound and to serve as first warning in the advent of military or police raids. He hoped the roadblock had been the only post, because if he met a coordinated attack coming from the other direction on the narrow road he knew they would never survive it.

A sudden turn appeared out of the rain he was forced to brake again, letting the Humvee pull closer. He made the turn and heard a burst of automatic gunfire from behind him. He cut into the turn, clawing for purchase, but he couldn't see well enough to judge the angle and accelerate into it so he was forced to apply his brakes once again.

The high beams of the Humvee were blinding spots in his rearview mirror and the big military vehicle was close enough now that Bolan could clearly hear the roar of its engine. He felt the continuous splash of falling rain through his open window, and the water ran in rivers off his windshield wipers.

He shot out of the curve and onto a straight stretch of road that plunged down the mountainside at a sharp angle. Several bullets buzzed through the truck followed by a streaking red tracer. They struck the windshield and blew it out.

Bolan threw up an arm as the gusting wind drove shards of glass into the cab of the vehicle. He felt the splinters of glass whip past his face, cutting at the exposed skin like angry biting flies.

He lowered his arm and a mound of earth suddenly appeared in the roadway in front of the truck. He had no time to avoid the mud slide; it had appeared too abruptly. The bumper smashed into the mud and debris exploded upward and outward. The truck cantered onto two wheels, then bounced roughly backward. For a single horrifying moment Bolan was sure the truck had become high centered. The vehicle teetered on top of the column of mud, wheels spinning for purchase.

Then the Humvee raced up behind them and crashed into the bumper. The impact threw Bolan and Sukarno-putri forward against the braces of their seat belts. Bolan felt his teeth snap together as his neck whiplashed.

He gasped at the sudden sharp pain of the restraint against his chest cranked the steering wheel. The battered truck spilled down the other side of the mud slide. The Humvee was in every way the superior vehicle, and it crashed into the truck for a second time.

The truck fishtailed as the engine raced in futile

protest. The Humvee raced over the top of the mud slide easily. Bolan gunned the engine, the purchase was too uncertain for his tires and he was slow. The Humvee struck the truck a third time.

The back end of the truck slid around in a tight arc, and Bolan found the nose of his vehicle pointed straight up the mountain. He gunned it and cranked his front wheels hard to his right in a desperate last attempt to find purchase.

Gravity pulled with inexorable force and Bolan felt the truck slide. Then the Humvee surged forward for a final time, ramming hard into the front of the cab. The trucked careened over the edge of the road and plunged down the mountainside.

7

Bolan had time to see a man lean far out of the passenger window of the Humvee's front door and spray at him with a P-90 submachine gun. Bullets riddled the hood of the truck and steam billowed upward but was beaten down by the pouring rain.

Bolan yanked up on the emergency brake, locking the rear wheels and then threw himself against the steering wheel to try to swing the front end of the vehicle around and gain some semblance of control.

The rear corner of the truck smacked into some unseen obstruction and Bolan's desperate gamble started to work. He goosed the gas pedal. His sharply cut wheel tore into the sliding earth, gripped and then pulled.

The vehicle spun and Bolan found himself pointed straight down hill. Sukarnoputri had fallen silent and that worried Bolan.

He found it was becoming easier to see and realized that there was less rain blowing into his face. Then he saw he'd been run off the road in a section of old-growth triple canopy. Ancient jungle giants stood in columns like pillars. The thick canopy was blocking the full force of the rain.

Bolan tapped his brakes and slalomed around an outcropping before threading the sliding truck between the trunks of two trees. The side mirror was ripped off his vehicle. He focused on onrushing obstacles. He spun the wheel gently, each turn exaggerated intensely by the constant landslides of soft earth under his spinning wheels, and dodged a fallen log. He fought the wheel back around to try to slide past a jutting tree stump as large as a parked car, but his tires could gain no purchase and he realized he was going to hit.

Bolan flung his arm out to try to cushion Sukarnoputri. The impact was deafening as the front hood crumpled upward and flew backward, covering the jagged hole of the front windshield.

Bolan was thrown hard against his set belt and he felt the soft, hot cushion of Sukarnoputri's body as the same thing happened to her. They both were jerked back into their seats by their restraints. The engine whined to shriek as a fan belt came loose and began slapping against metal.

Dazed and hurt, Bolan reached out and switched off the ignition. The engine rattled to a stop before anything could catch fire, and the soldier reached across to release his seat belt. He undid the restraint and looked over at Sukarnoputri as he felt around for the Beretta.

The Indonesian woman hung limply in her harness. She did not move or utter a sound. Bolan leaned forward and reached to pull the woman's arm out of her lap to feel for a pulse. His hand came away wet.

Her pulse beat erratically and shallow, much the way she was breathing. She slumped in the ruined seat, unconscious. Bolan let her go and tried to find his pistol. Behind and above him the spotlight from the Humvee swept down across the topography, hunting the landscape.

Bolan kicked open his door after clicking off the dome light. The fighters in the Humvee would be coming down the mountain to hunt for him, he had no doubt. Sukarnoputri's only chance lay in Bolan drawing the killers into the jungle and finishing them off. He had lost his weapon in the crash, and he began searching for the silenced Beretta.

He tumbled out of the ruined truck and knelt in the mud and rain outside the driver door. He leaned into the vehicle and quickly ran his hands along the floorboards and under the seat, searching for the handgun.

He saw the spotlight cycle past the truck again and knew that the trail of the truck's passage down the hillside had to be obvious; a veritable road map of churned earth, broken branches and scraped tree bark. Soon the searching eye of the spotlight would find the evidence and the killers would start down after them.

Unable to find his pistol Bolan stood. Time was running out. From up the hill he heard voices suddenly shout in excited tones and he knew his respite was over.

He cast about him for something to use, anything to even the odds. For no other reason than desperation he remembered the five-gallon jerri cans he had seen kept in the back of the original vehicle he had stolen from the terror or criminal cell.

If one group vehicle had been outfitted in that matter, then why not more? Bolan ran to the back of the truck. A spare tire had been mounted on the rear hatch, and Bolan could see how it had served as makeshift armor, absorbing bullets and deflecting them off the metal hub of the wheel.

He leaned in and looked in the back of the truck. He saw a tire jack and a small metal toolbox, and next to that the answer to his prayers. He reached in and pulled the gas can free from the black rubber bungee cord holding it in place. He wasted no time in spinning the cap free of the mouth.

Unceremoniously he upended the can, spreading the gas in a pool the shape of a crescent moon around the back of the wrecked truck. He quickly ran a trail to a jungle cypress, which provided at least initial cover.

From up above he heard an angry man barking orders and then an answer from someone surprisingly close. Bolan grimaced. He had hoped to pull Sukarnoputri's unconscious body from the truck before initiating his trap, but their pursuers were too close.

He settled into the lee of the jungle cypress and pulled a lighter from his pocket.

The spotlight cut across the forest and settled on the roof of the truck. Streaks of rain could bee seen running off the tree canopy and dropping down through the illumination. The solid beam of light stayed locked into position, and Bolan closed one eye against its glare to save his night vision.

After a moment he heard heavy footfalls. The incline was too sharp for silent stalking, and the gunmen from the Humvee were stumbling down the mountain. Loose rocks tumbled toward the crumpled truck, and the hunter came into sight.

Crouched tightly in the lee of the trunk Bolan tensed, ready with his lighter. He silently urged the man to hurry his approach before dripping rainwater diluted his gasoline puddle.

The hunter held a P-90 submachine gun at the ready. He moved in a sideways shuffle to avoid slipping. Bolan watched him draw closer to the wreck. He was gambling on the man's trigger control, that the Indonesian gunner wouldn't simply spray the vehicle before checking it, that the terror cell still wanted the two interlopers alive if possible. He had no choice, given his current armament but to take that risk.

The man slid into the kill zone and Bolan sprung his trap.

He thumbed the lighter, which sparked on the first strike. Bolan brought the flame near the toe of his right boot.

Registering the sudden flash of light the hunter turned toward Bolan's position, his weapon muzzle swinging up. Bolan touched his flame to the trail of gasoline and it ignited. The hunter finished his spin and sank to one knee, the stock of the P-90 finding the hollow of his shoulder.

A trail of flame sprang up between the two combatants, and Bolan rolled away behind the heavy trunk of the tree. He rolled out on the other side, uphill from the tree just as the flames reached the kneeling hunter. The puddled gas went up like a time bomb around the suddenly screaming man.

Bolan was up and sprinting forward as if he were cutting through the line of scrimmage on a football field. Panicked, the blazing gunman turned to run up the hill and out of the pool of fire. He slipped and went down then screamed in a wretched, agonized choke as his hair caught ablaze.

Bolan sprang into the air in a modified leaping sidekick. The tread of his combat boot caught the man square in his chest and the two went down. Bolan felt heat blaze up around him as he passed through the sheet of flame.

He landed hard on the ground of the incline and bounced up to land against the back of the truck. The gunman rolled around at his feet, struck dumb by the blow, his clothing still burning. Bolan spun and scooped up the P-90 submachine gun that had been torn free of the Indonesian's grasp.

His finger found the trigger and he silenced the tortured man's scream with a point-blank burst. He was out of the sight of the men above him because of the wall of flame and he capitalized on that by running into the woods beside the burning fire and throwing himself to the ground behind a fallen tree.

Bolan scanned the hillside above him. He quickly pinpointed the parked Humvee with its door-mounted spotlight. He thumbed the selector switch on the P-90 to single shot and carefully aimed the weapon toward the blinding center of the searchlight.

He closed one eye against the glare and gently exhaled through his nose, ignoring the seeping dampness of the wet earth beneath him. His finger closed around the smooth metal curve of the trigger as he disregarded the fetid stink of jungle rot.

The P-90 jumped in his hand, his trigger pull so smooth the round detonation almost came as a surprise. Instantly the spotlight winked out in a shower of sparks. Panicked gunfire raked the jungle in response, coming nowhere near the prone Bolan. The gas fire began to die down as the fuel was consumed and the incessant rain worked its inevitable conclusion.

Bolan fired another careful round toward the muzzle-flash coming from next to the Humvee. The harassing fire stopped. Bolan used the lull to change position. He waited, carefully watching the road above him for the slightest opportunity to take a shot.

He was acutely aware of how long Sukarnoputri had been left by herself, alone and bleeding. He began to inch back toward the wreck of the truck.

Above he saw headlights suddenly flare on and heard the roar of the Humvee engine as someone revved the gas pedal. Bolan threw himself down and swept up his submachine gun. The Humvee lurched backward, tires spinning and Bolan began to pump rounds at the vehicle as he realized it was in full flight.

He saw his 5.7 mm rounds spark off the framework of the Humvee's body to little effect. The heavy vehicle pulled back from the edge of the road, and then the driver sped away, fleeing the scene.

Bolan eased his finger off the trigger of his weapon. For now the battle was over, and he had driven his opponents from the field. He was sure the driver had fled in search of reinforcements, but if they were expected to come from the mining compound he would find his headquarters in chaos.

Bolan slung the P-90 across his body where it could hang in easy reach. He rose quickly and navigated the steep hillside toward the truck.

The fire had died down to flickering blue-yellow flames that cast long shadows on the vehicle's dented body. He approached the window on the passenger side and looked in.

Sukarnoputri's head hung limply and she remained unmoving in her seat harness. Bolan grabbed the door handle in both hands and jerked the abused structure open. It came apart from the main frame with a violent screeching. Bolan leaned in and pulled the woman's seat belt from her. She looked ghastly in the flickering flame of the gasoline fire.

Bolan pulled her out of the vehicle and placed her on the ground. The blood that had pooled in her lap spilled out, running across Bolan's arms and shirtfront. He checked her pulse and was relieved to find one.

He rose and rushed around the truck to where he had put his field pack. The bag felt unbearably heavy to him and he realized just how exhausted he was after his harrowing succession of ordeals.

He came back around the truck and threw the pack down on the ground. He went to a knee and began to rummage through it, spilling what he needed across the ground while rain dripped down on him from the interlocked branches above his head.

He moved quickly to place his pressure dressing on the main wounds in Sukarnoputri's shoulder, abdomen and upper thigh. Even as he staunched the bleeding and bound her wounds, he realized how badly she needed emergency medical care. She was going to die without help, and nothing he could do would change that fact.

Bolan conducted an internal debate. Scrubbing his mission was unthinkable to the Executioner. Sukarnoputri was his contact, a means to an end. But she had suffered greatly since coming to Bolan's aid, and her life now lay in his hands.

He had hard choices to make, and if Sukarnoputri was going to live then he needed to be making them quickly. He knew he couldn't call for extraction. In the current downpour a helicopter rescue was impossible.

Sukarnoputri needed medical help and quickly. There was only one place in the immediate vicinity that had access to medical supplies and automobiles. If Bolan wanted to save the Indonesian woman, he would have to return to the terrorist compound.

He worked quickly. First he used his knife to strip the seat covers off the ruined truck, then he used his parachute rappel ribbon—intended for tree or cliff landings—to rig up a drag. He pulled the unconscious Sukarnoputri up the hill and across the logging road to the lee of a fallen tree where he rigged the rest of the seat cover as a blind to keep the rain off her.

It was far from perfect, and it gnawed at Bolan to know he was leaving a critically injured comrade in such a fashion. But cold-blooded assessments and strength of his convictions were the fuel Bolan had always used to see him through his long ordeals.

If Sukarnoputri was going to die, then she would die. But if she could be saved, Bolan would move heaven and earth to try. Once the injured woman was as reasonably comfortable as he could make her, he set out up the road toward the terror camp.

He jogged out into the middle of the road and began to double-time up the center of the lane. He wasn't worried about being surprised by vehicles as he was sure he would see them coming long before they realized he was there. And there was no time for him to take the safer but slower route of paralleling the road.

He figured he was a half hour by foot down the road from the camp, moving up hill in the rain. He ran at a steady jog, with a loose grip on his submachine gun to conserve energy. His rhythm was constantly being challenged by deep ruts, potholes and broken ground on the road. Despite the rain he sweated freely from the exertion in the tropical climate.

He had to get to the compound and steal another vehicle at the very least if not outright try to raid the site's medical facility. He put his head down against the rain, determined to save a life.

8

Smoke hung low around the site, beaten into submission by the humidity. The charred skeletons of buildings stood smoldering in the downpour. There was no obvious movement as the Executioner scanned the compound.

The structures that had formed the administration site had been destroyed by his satchel charges and the resulting fire. There were no vehicles at the site, and Bolan realized that if he wanted to gather what he needed he was going to have to penetrate the main mine itself.

He thought about its; narrow twisting halls, steep staircases, and warren of boxlike rooms. He didn't relish the idea of a return to the dark labyrinth.

He melted back into the jungle and began making his way uphill. The old-growth trees had been knocked down toward the top of the little mountain and underbrush had grown in thick. Bamboo stands punctuated the thick bush, and clinging vines forcing Bolan to pick his way carefully through the dark.

At the crest of the mountain Bolan saw the Humvee parked in front of the mine housing. It had been shut off and sat silent before the doors. The corpse of the sentry Bolan had been forced to kill to make his escape lay facedown in a growing puddle of rain water.

The door into the mine building hung open.

Bolan was well-aware that military Humvees were not key operated. The ignition was controlled by a thumb lever set into the dash next to the steering wheel. He could simply take the military vehicle and make an escape. Other than a dinosaur of an old truck, there were no other vehicles.

He quickly assessed the situation. Sukarnoputri needed more than the makeshift medical attention Bolan had given her. She needed better bandages, IV fluids, painkillers and, in this tropical environment, antibiotics. Bolan knew from his search for her that the first-floor equipment room had supplies of those things.

He adjusted his grip on his submachine gun leading the way. He was thirsty and his body was sore from the abuse he had taken. He studied the front gate to the building's parking area for a long moment, then rose.

He covered the ground, moving fast, his submachine gun leading the way. He angled his approach so that the bulky frame of the Humvee was between himself and the front door of the building. He jogged through the front gate and onto the worn and broken asphalt.

The soldier reached the rear corner of the Humvee

and moved up the side of the vehicle, still using it as cover from the building. He kept the P-90 up as he reached out with his left hand and worked the handle of the rear door, opening it.

He ducked, leading with the muzzle of his submachine gun, finger poised on the trigger. He scanned the dark interior. Trash littered the floorboards and the cab smelled of unwashed bodies, but it was empty.

He quickly leaned into the vehicle and searched for a first-aid kit but found nothing. He looked up through the Humvee windshield toward the mine entrance. The door still hung open, motionless. Rain ran in rivers of the windshield. He saw no lights or movement from the silent building.

Bolan pulled back out of the vehicle and softly closed the door. There was no cover on his approach to the mine entrance; he would be exposed the entire way. Thirty yards would seem like a marathon under fire.

He swept the P-90 into position in the lee of his shoulder and broke from around the edge of the Humvee, covering the ground fast, splashing through puddles as he ran. He came up to the doorway and twisted to put his back to the wall beside the entrance.

The soldier went down to one knee beside the open door then swung around the edge of the door frame. He saw an empty antechamber, sandbag-lined walls and coat racks. The floor was littered with crushed cigarette butts.

The Executioner rose and shuffled through the

doorway. He immediately shifted to one side and swept the muzzle of the submachine gun around, clearing sectors quickly. He found nothing and stopped to take stock of his situation. In the corner of the room was the door to the hall he had come down to make his original escape. He could hear nothing.

He crossed the room and quickly scanned around the corner before snatching his head back. The hall ran for a short way before turning the corner. It was empty. Bolan shifted around the corner and began to make his approach walking heel-toe in careful steps, weapon up.

He came to the turn in the hall leading to the stairs down to the working levels. He cleared the corner in a methodical manner, then began his approach, noting the corpses of the sentries he had killed earlier. Without interference he made his way to the door to the equipment room.

He kept his cheek sealed to the butt of his weapon, both eyes open as he reached out for the doorknob. He grabbed it and twisted quickly before jerking the door open and stepping across the threshold.

He scanned the room, poised to shoot. He saw the damage from before, the dead men on the floor, the overturned chair. He let the door close behind him, then placed a second chair in front of it to give him extra warning should anyone try to enter.

He cocked his arm and maintained his hold on the P-90 by the pistol grip, his finger resting on the trigger. Quickly, disregarding the mess, Bolan began to toss the equipment room. In a white cabinet set in brackets on the wall next to the weapons rack he found what he was looking for and quickly stuffed supplies into various pockets.

He turned to leave. Crossing the room, he moved the chair out of the way and pulled the door open.

He stepped out into the poorly lit hallway and let the door swing shut behind him. He looked down the hall toward the front of the building and saw nothing. He turned and observed the long stretch of hall leading back toward the staircase. He saw the heavy metal door was closed. He let out his pent-up breath in a smooth rush. The window set in the door showed only darkness.

The door to the staircase suddenly swung open on the hydraulic-enhanced hinges and a man stepped through. He was dressed in a green rain jacket that was slick and shiny with moisture. He wore blue jeans tucked into mud-splattered canvas-and-leather jungle boots. The hood of his jacket was thrown back, revealing an Indonesian man with a shaved head. A hand-rolled cigarette dangled from thin, bloodless lips in the gloomy light of the hall.

The man's eyes widened in surprise, then narrowed. He held an M-4 carbine with a drum-magazine attachment in his hands. His lips twisted in snarl and the cigarette tumbled down. It struck the front of his rain jacket and a shower of sparks fanned out. He swung up the muzzle of the carbine.

Bolan twisted at the hips, leveling his own weapon

as the man crouched into the shoulder stock of his carbine. Bolan threw himself backward and pulled the trigger on his submachine gun.

The M-4 chattered as the man fired. Bolan had time to register the yellow muzzle-flashed and sensed the deadly lead projectiles cutting through the stale air of the hallway directly in front of him.

Bolan's P-90 bucked as he fired, and he saw his rounds punch into the green plastic material of the man's jacket a heartbeat before the ragged holes poured red in fountain streams. The man stumbled backward and triggered another burst of his own. A red tracer burned down the hall past Bolan.

The Executioner readied his weapon and squeezed the trigger again. A second 3-round burst caught the Indonesian gunman, this time in the throat and jaw. Blood splashed like paint across the wall, and the metal door as the man was shoved backward.

The M-4 dropped from the man's hands and tumbled to the ground with a rattle. The man bounced off the door and fell forward. His throat was a jagged wound of exposed flesh, and his jawbone had been shattered by one of Bolan's armor-piercing 5.7 mm rounds.

The gunman struck the floor with a heavy, wet sound and sprawled out dead. Bolan looked for a moment at the corpse, then lowered his smoking weapon.

He moved quickly, navigating the hall and lobby before exiting the mine and crossing the parking lot. The rain hadn't let up during the short time he was in the building and he was soaked again almost instantly. He jogged over to the Humvee and slid behind the wheel. He fed the engine gas and turned the ignition over. The engine roared to life.

Bolan pulled his captured cell phone from a pocket and checked his reception as he turned the Humvee in a tight circle and drove out of the mine's parking lot. The huge vehicle tore down the dirt road easily navigating the torn up surface. Bolan cranked up the windshield wipers and turned on his high beams. It was a calculated risk. He thought most survivors of his attack would recognize the vehicle as one of their own and without his night-vision goggles, he had no hope of staying on the road in any case without the headlights.

Unsurprisingly, the captured field commander's cell phone didn't have coverage in the inclement weather and remote location. He would have to wait until he could get to his sat-com unit in his pack before he tried to make contact with Grimaldi and his support elements.

According to his briefing, Grimaldi and Mott had clearances to secure a platform on a U.S. Navy vessel.

From that platform in the Strait of Malacca and other points in the South China Sea, Stony Man Farm was prepared to operate logistical support for Bolan's Indonesian mission. If ever he needed logistical support it was now, he realized. Grimaldi would put a helicopter down wherever Bolan wanted, but not in this weather and only after communications were established.

His plan was, as circumstances dictated, simple. He would gather Sukarnoputri and return to the abandoned airstrip he had inserted on. He would treat the woman's wounds while gaining contact with Grimaldi. The old airfield would provide a good landing zone for helicopter extraction. It was problematic in that it had already been compromised once, but Bolan didn't know the area and had no other choices, especially with his contact stringer too injured to help him.

He clocked a mile away from the compound on the Humvee's odometer, then slowed the military vehicle, scanning his surroundings to find the place where he had left Sukarnoputri. He drove another five minutes, dropping his speed in steady increments as he drew closer to the sight of the truck wreck and the subsequent gun battle with the Humvee's original occupants.

Finally he was able to spot the still smoldering but flameless wreck of the truck and resulting scar to the jungle topography. He stopped the Humvee, left it running and jumped out into the rain.

He cut across the hillside moving fast. He found Sukarnoputri just where he had left her. He saw how wan and wasted the young woman looked. The butchers of humanity had struck again and another innocent had paid the price. It was painfully obvious that she was close to death.

Bolan tucked his submachine gun behind his back on its sling and bent next to the Indonesian woman. He gathered her light body into his arms and lifted her from the ground. She was shivering almost uncontrollably, and her body was flushed and hot from fever to his touch.

He cut back down the short stretch of hillside toward the Humvee. He opened the back door on the driver side and arranged Sukarnoputri's limp body as best he could.

He climbed back behind the wheel of the Humvee and put the military into drive. His mind spun as he came up with options, considered their merits and then disregarded them. He ran out of options very quickly.

Sukarnoputri was the only contact he had. He was alone and isolated in a remote and rugged area of an unfamiliar country. His only asset was gravely wounded, and he had been put through a ringer himself. Everything that could go wrong on a clandestine insertion seemed to *have* gone wrong. He was isolated from support by inclement weather.

After being on the ground for several hours and surviving a multitude of ordeals he was being forced to return to his starting point. So far in Indonesia all the Executioner had been able to accomplish was running in circles.

He set his face in a grim mask and pushed the Humvee through the driving rain back up the road where he and Sukarnoputri had originally been ambushed. He could only hope that once he got to the hangar his sat-com phone would reach Stony Man Farm and Jack Grimaldi.

9

The Executioner found the old airfield by process of elimination and managed to pull the Humvee up onto the feeder road by backtracking along his original route and using his GPS unit with his original LZ coordinates as a guide.

He shot around the old rusted metal pole that served as a barrier and drove the Humvee out onto the broken asphalt of the forgotten runway. Standing puddles of water from the still pouring rain had filled up the cracks and potholes of the once smoothly paved strip. He was forced to slow the Humvee further to avoid jolting and jerking the still unconscious Sukarnoputri into a more serious state.

The powerful headlights of the Humvee illuminated the front of the dark hangar as Bolan pulled up to the hanging gate and damaged fence. Leaving the headlights fixed on the building, Bolan climbed out of the vehicle.

He left the engine running and the Humvee's door open. He pulled the P-90 submachine gun to him and walked out into the rain. He shoved the damaged gate all the way open, then got back into the vehicle and pulled inside the fence. He threw the vehicle into park again and got out to reinspect the hangar, which loomed large above the front end of the vehicle.

Using the Humvee headlights for illumination, he approached the hangar door. He jerked the door open, the headlights casting his shadow out long and distorted across the oil-stained concrete floor. He looked around carefully, ignoring the growing sodden weight of his clothes as the rain hammered down into him.

Satisfied, Bolan returned to the Humvee, climbed in and drove the vehicle inside the hangar. Once he had maneuvered the military vehicle inside the structure, he shut off the lights, hopped out and yanked the sliding door closed again behind him. For a moment he had found shelter from the elements and a primitive sanctuary for his wounded comrade. He needed to make contact with his support quickly.

He went to the back passenger door of the Humvee and opened it. From the deep foot well behind the front seat he manhandled his backpack clear and tore it open.

There were several bullet holes in the pack and a long tear along the back where stray enemy rounds had been absorbed by his kit. The potential trouble this could cause him was evident, and after a brief search he found his sat-com phone.

An enemy round had cracked the phone in two and spread its shattered circuitry around the bag's main compartment. Bolan snarled in frustration and shoved the pack away from him. His only hope of contact was the captured cell phone he had taken from the field commander at the mining compound.

He began to reach for the phone. Sukarnoputri lifted her head inside the back of the Humvee and began to cough violently. Bolan looked up. Bright pink blood poured out of the woman's mouth and leaked down her face. He leaped to his feet as she began to choke.

He reached the woman and turned her head to the side to let the blood spill out before she could continue to aspirate on it. Long ropes of bloody salvia rolled out from the injured woman's slack lips. Her fever warmed Bolan's grip as he held her head and a heavy sheen of perspiration covered her pale skin.

She sputtered once as Bolan held her, then spasmed in his hands. Just like that the frantic rise and fall of her chest ceased.

"No!" Bolan shouted.

He reached under Sukarnoputri's arms and pulled her clear of the vehicle. He saw that the pressure dressing he had put on her thigh had soaked through and that blood had leaked through on her back as well, leaving his hands crimson.

He set her down carefully. He tilted her head back, then lifted her chin to clear her airway. He leaned in close, pressing his ear to her blood-tinged lips to listen and feel for breath while he watched her chest, hoping for a rise and fall. He was rewarded with neither.

His fingers went to her neck, searching for a pulse, and again he found nothing. Sukarnoputri's heart had ceased beating. Bolan moved into position over the woman's still body.

He covered her mouth with his own. She tasted like blood, and he could still smell the lingering trace of her perfume. One hand found the curve at the back of her neck while the other pinched shut her nostrils. Slowly he exhaled his breath down her throat and watched for the rise and fall of her chest. He lowered his head and repeated the procedure.

He found her sternum and placed the palm of his hand on it two inches above the Xiphoid Process. He laced the fingers of his other hand together with the first and began doing chest compressions. He found his rhythm and began performing his CPR cycles with mechanical efficiency.

"Come on," he whispered.

His own breathing became labored as if he was running a race. The cartilage along her ribcage *snapped* and *popped* as he worked. He considered the grisly sounds as signs of progress and kept pushing.

Sukarnoputri's sternum compressed and expanded under Bolan's weight as he worked, forcing her still heart to pump oxygenated blood through her body. He knew how infrequently CPR alone, without the intervention of advanced life support techniques worked and he knew he couldn't keep working on an unresponsive body forever. If she didn't respond soon he'd be forced to give up.

He worked in silence except for the sound of his own exertion and the continuous rhythm of rain falling on the roof of the old hangar.

"Come on," he repeated.

An exhausted ache had settled into the tensed muscles of his arms and shoulders, and he had begun to perspire freely. Hope faded in direct, inverse proportion to his fatigue.

Sukarnoputri remained inert under his efforts. Finally he snarled his frustration and changed tactics.

He lifted his right fist above his head and slammed it on the woman's chest at the junction of the middle and lower third of her sternum. He lifted his fist and did it again. The blows made dull, hollow sounds that echoed weirdly under the initial smack of flesh on flesh. Each time he slammed his fist down the woman's body shivered under the impact.

Sukarnoputri jerked under his hands like a woman in a seizure. She opened her mouth and coughed violently. A bloody spray of phlegm struck Bolan's cheek and he wiped at it with a grungy sleeve as he turned to look down at the woman.

Sukarnoputri breathed. He cradled the woman's head in his lap and watched her. Her eyelids fluttered, but she never opened them. Slowly her breathing evened out and Bolan eased her back down onto ground, making her as comfortable as he could.

Once he had finished arranging the unconscious woman he again pulled out the cell phone he had taken from the field commander at the mining compound. He knew he had little hope of getting a signal, but the old landing strip was at the top of the jungle mountain and the increase in elevation might make all the difference.

Miraculously he got a signal. He noted how low on juice the phone was and hoped it would last long enough for him to complete his system negotiations. The relay station, serving as a gatekeeper, requested a code number and Bolan gave it. Once he had been admitted into the protective technology Bolan used its surrogate links to enter Stony Man communications, then dialed the number to the sat phone Jack Grimaldi used while in the field.

There was a long momentum as Bolan listened to the phone ringing. Finally the line was answered and he felt relief wash over him.

"This is Grimaldi," Jack answered. "Go ahead."

"Jack, this is me," Bolan answered.

"Goddamn it!" Grimaldi bellowed. "We've been trying to get hold of you for hours!"

"I know, I've run into difficulties." Bolan said. "I think I'm going to need an extraction. My stringer is down and hurt."

"Yes, you do have problems, old buddy. Listen up,

we've got some difficulties of our own. It seems our Stringer was nabbed some time ago by the Indonesian internal security service. They put a bug on her somehow to monitor her dealings with foreign intelligence."

"Beautiful," Bolan muttered.

"It gets worse," Grimaldi agreed. "Seems they're using the woman as a stalking horse to get at you. You've been marked."

"We've already been hit. It explains a lot of things. Look, I'm at our original LZ. I need you to come get me once the rain lets up. It'll have to be by helicopter, though. The runway is too ripped up."

"That's the problem," Grimaldi said. His voice sounded strained. "The woman must still have a beacon on her. The NSA picked up traffic of a unit scrambling to get you. We recognized the coordinates right away. Zamira's hitters were on their way almost half an hour ago. Apparently some wild-eyed gunman blew up a covert training camp and pissed off rogue government elements."

Bolan grunted. He reached up and began rubbing his temples. His forehead had begun to throb.

"You're telling me an assault force is coming here?" Bolan said.

"Yes, you've got get out."

"The woman is too badly wounded," Bolan said. "The trip here almost killed her. If I move her again she dies. Can you get us out?"

"We've got another problem," Grimaldi said.

"What?"

"We're not at war with Indonesia. These may be rogue elements of the government, but they're still *government*. The Man has put the quash on getting you out if it means shooting at Indonesians. That means the commander here is under orders not to help me out. No helicopter, no indirect fire, nothing. I'm free to leave with the plane I flew in on, but his hands are tied."

"I can't leave her to die, and if I move her she dies," Bolan said.

"She's dead anyway. She's already been made. If you hit the jungle, you can make it out," Grimaldi said.

"You know I'm not going to do that," Bolan replied.

The Stony Man pilot paused on the other end of the line. "Yeah, I know. I was just hoping you'd see some sense *this* time."

"I made her a promise, I'm going to keep it if I can," Bolan said.

"Look, I don't care how bad she is. Get her back in your vehicle and drive," Grimaldi suggested.

"There's only one road in or out of this area. If they're rolling hot now, I'm already in trouble."

"Listen," Grimaldi's voice almost broke. "You know Hal and Barb won't stand for this. They'll find a way to reason with the Man."

"Plausible deniability," Bolan said. "The nation needs this kept quiet, and that means I'm expendable. I knew that going in. The Man isn't going to change his mind."

"Damn it, I'm not giving up!" Grimaldi snarled into the phone.

"You got this number in your phone now?" Bolan asked.

"Yeah."

"If anything changes, let me know," Bolan said. "Otherwise I've got to start throwing up some defenses."

"As soon as this low pressure front recedes enough to get my plane in the air, we'll figure something out. You made that woman a promise, and now I'm going to make you one. No matter what I'm going to help you."

"Be careful, Jack."

"You're telling *me* to be careful?" Grimaldi laughed.

"Call me if the weather changes," Bolan said.

"You hang on. I will find a way," Grimaldi promised.

"I trust you. I'm out." Bolan hung up before the conversation became even more difficult.

He looked down at the unconscious Sukarnoputri. Her color wasn't good, but she looked at peace. He remembered her begging him to help her see her baby again.

He stood, sliding the phone away. His mind raced through options. Flight was out. It was as he'd pointed out to Grimaldi—there was only a single road, and the fragile Sukarnoputri was in no shape to make any journey without intensive medical support. For the same reason he couldn't cut through the jungle to try to escape and evade from the coming units of gunmen.

The Executioner was going to be making a last stand.

He went to the wounded woman and began shaking her down. He was experienced enough in the duplicitous ways of modern government agents that he found the tracking device quickly.

He used his knife to carve it out of the heel of her shoe, then crushed it under the tread of his own boot. It made a satisfying *crunch* as he ground it into the floor of the hangar. His satisfaction was short-lived, however.

Men with guns were coming for him.

He began to take stock of his situation. In the military it was called an "ACE report." It meant simply Ammunition, Causalities and Equipment.

His weaponry was limited to his stolen P-90 and a handful of 50-round clips. The FN P-90 was an outstanding weapon, but it was insignificant in the face of automatic weapons, rocket launchers and significant numbers.

He was beat up and banged about but ambulatory. The woman was in extremely poor condition, and he knew the slightest shock could stop her heart again.

He had a dying cell phone, a satchel charge, an empty hangar and a decades-old Humvee low on gas and short on armor upgrades.

He went to the Humvee and opened the back, really searching in earnest for everything the vehicle might contain that could help him.

He had to adapt, improvise, overcome—the very motto of the United States infantry forces. He moved to the front door, opened it enough to keep one eye on what was happening outside and then began to shake the Humvee down.

The first things he found were tools—a shovel, pick, double bladed ax, and a long pry bar. The communications gear had been stripped out of the vehicle's dash. Under a seat he found a lug wrench and jack for changing a tire. In a similar compartment under the driver's seat he found a ratchet set.

Other than that, the Humvee contained nothing but mud and trash. Bolan turned and looked around the cavernous hangar, which was stark and empty. There was the dented body of an soda machine, its face dark next to the hangar door. The landing strip had not been a commercial operation so there was no office, only a single bathroom with a grungy old toilet long since drained, and a dirty sink without running water.

Working quickly he cleaned the room as best he could, then moved Sukarnoputri into the small space. He tried to insulate her against loss of her body heat. He retied her bandages, then elevated her feet about ten inches off the ground to ease the strain on her already over worked heart.

He left the office, then checked the front of the building. He saw no sign of the approaching forces as the rain continued to beat down. He emptied his backpack next to the Humvee, then took it and the shovel outside the front door. He moved rapidly, shoveling mud into the empty main pouch until it was filled.

He lugged the pack back inside and place the impromptu sandbag barrier in front of the closed door to the bathroom where he had placed Sukarnoputri.

He walked over to the front door of the hangar and yanked it closed, dropping the latch into place. He tipped over the ancient soda machine. It landed in front of the hangar door forming a three-foot barrier.

Bolan stepped back and wiped the sweat from his forehead.

Streaks of white light appeared out of the dark and rain, sweeping bars of illumination into the black hangar through the broken windows and casting wild shadows. He heard the throaty growl of powerful engines and retrieved the P-90 submachine gun.

The killers had arrived.

10

Hal Brognola sat in his office and looked outside at the gray water of the Potomac. He held his phone against his ear and listened as Barbara Price told him the sudden, surprising information that had come out of the Indonesian situation.

"You're certain?" he asked. "The numbers are the same? There's no mistake? I'll tell the Man, then."

Brognola slowly leaned over and hung up his phone. What he had learned was horrible, but at the same time it had given him ammunition with which he could fight for asset support for his long-time friend.

A woman was missing.

A woman was missing and political expediency had come down on the side letting it remain a mystery. Those sworn to her protection had weighted the scales of national interest and turned their backs. There was angst in the betrayal because her superiors were good people, but political decisions often rush over the individual with impersonal power.

Hal Brognola though about all the pieces of the puzzle.

Indonesian shipping magnate Zamira Loebis has been the subject of American government and Interpol investigations for more than two decades. He had been linked to all forms of illicit trafficking with his vast fleet of modern ships, including narcotics, people and weapons. Eight years earlier he'd used his fortune to move into the realm of influence-peddling on the world stage.

He began serving as a middleman between wealthy leaders of rogue states and interested businessmen in first tier economies. His purchase of a cluster of jungle atolls in international waters off the coast of Malaysia immediately set off alarms in the State Department.

The State Department sent a team of agents to Brunei to investigate. The team consisted of two investigators and a four-man team of agents from the Diplomatic Security Service. One week into the investigation all communication abruptly ended. Two days later the bodies of the DSS team washed up on the shores of Brunei.

A flurry of activity initially galvanized the U.S. government. Then word came from the embassies of both Brunei and Malaysia that they would prefer the matter be handled as a internal security issue by their respective national agencies. In return both countries would sign antiterrorism treaties designed to blunt the spread of extremism in their respective communities. The matter was officially reclassified as a liaison incident.

The lives of the few were sacrificed for the lives of

the many, and it was hard to argue that it wouldn't lead to a reduction in the influence of terror leaders in a region already rife with killing in the name of religion.

But one of the dead State Department agents, Helene Burke, happened to be the daughter of a former governor of Virginia. Her father was also an old friend of Brognola's. The distraught politician had called in a favor, and Brognola had sent Mack Bolan.

However, the possession of the woman's cell phone by an Indonesian government death squad leader had shifted the balance of power. The delicate political fencing match had shifted, and the Oval Office could more fully flex its international muscle while still demanding legitimate assistance.

The man from Justice decided such political vagaries may have become a lifeline for the embattled Mack Bolan.

He picked up his phone to alert Jack Grimaldi.

THE EXECUTIONER MOVED QUICKLY to the windows set on either side of the hangar door. He stayed back in the shadows of the left-hand opening and counted his enemies. Eight pickup trucks and SUVs pulled onto the potholed and cracked landing strip and raced toward the hangar.

The lead vehicles pulled out to wing positions forming a reverse-wedge phalanx formation that quickly merged into a semicircle across the old tarmac. Bolan held his fire, watching the assault play out.

The vehicles stopped, and men in civilian clothing poured from the cabs. He saw the same mixture of M-4 carbines and P-90 submachine guns he had seen at the mining compound. Four of the men moved to the back of two trucks and let the gates down. Immediately massive, black furred Alsatians dogs dropped to the ground, lips turned back to reveal wolflike incisors.

Civilian clothes, not uniforms. Carbines and SMGs, not machine guns and crew-served automatic weapons. Attack dogs, not grenade launchers. Light skinned vehicles instead of armored personnel carriers. What Bolan was seeing quickly added up.

They had sent a militia death squad after him, not official police or military units.

Death squads were often, but not exclusively, associated with the violent political repression of dictatorships, totalitarian states and similar regimes. The Indonesians were no different. Death squads typically had the tacit or express support of the state and comprised a secret police force, paramilitary group or official government unit with members drawn from the military or the police.

Death squads could be distinguished from terrorist groups by the fact that their violent actions were used to maintain the power of a local or national ruling party, rather than to disrupt existing authority structures.

Bolan watched as pairs of gunmen began flanking the

hangar by skirting the edge of the jungle. The only opening in the old hangar was at the front. The Quonset hut structure was vulnerable to fire directed through the walls, but those combatants would have no avenues of egress.

The Executioner had a plan that depended split-second timing to a nearly suicidal degree, but it was the only thing he could do. He had to bloody the death squad's nose badly enough and fend them off long enough for the rain to break. He knew his chances were slim.

He watched the gunmen take up their positions. Several moved into defensive positions along the line of vehicles, putting the hangar door in their gun sights.

They would try to kill him; he would try to stop them.

It was kill or be killed.

A balaclava-clad commander snarled an order and two gunmen triggered bursts of harassing fire through the broken windows by the hangar door. Bolan ducked from the burst, and they sailed harmlessly into the dark space of the structure to rattle off the far walls.

Immediately Bolan realized what the commander had been trying to accomplish. The shards of broken glass ringing the dark, open squares of the windows had been knocked down by the bursts, clearing the openings.

The field commander shouted once more, and the handlers jerked the leashes on the dogs. Two men stepped forward from behind the safety of a white pickup truck. Their submachine guns had been outfitted with flashlight attachments below the barrels. In unison the men clicked the lights on and narrowed their beams.

They began stalking toward the hangar, their powerful little flashlights cutting sharp beams of illumination through the gloom and falling rain. The gunman's faces were hidden behind the anonymous covers of balaclavas.

Here we go. Bolan thought grimly.

He watched the death squad members approach from the deep shadows beyond the broken window. He saw them nod toward each other once they passed the gate of the chain-link fence. They peeled off and headed for the windows on either side of the main door.

Bolan skidded into position. He crouched just to the left and below the windowsill, poised to strike. The gunman on the right reached his window first and shone his light across the dark hangar. It played across the cavernous space and ran over the silent form of the Humvee.

Just above Bolan the second gunman appeared. His light joined the first man's as his torso filled the window. The Executioner rose in flash. The man flinched as Bolan appeared, his eyes growing wide. The gunman tried to shift and bring his submachine gun to bear.

For a second the two men struggled hard, muscle against muscle in hand-to-hand combat. The Indonesian fought with the desperate strength of the terrified, and Bolan battled him with all the force of a predator.

Bolan snapped out his left hand and caught the forward leaning killer behind the neck, knocking him off his feet and pulling him through the window. The big American thrust the muzzle of his P-90 into the gunman's face and triggered a burst.

The Executioner twisted and heaved, yanking the dead man fully into the hangar through the window. Even as the corpse flopped to the ground Bolan stepped out from the wall and thrust his submachine gun out like a pistol, triggering a second burst.

The first death squad gunman screamed as his weapon shattered in his hands, then a wild round tore out his throat and he fell away, pumping blood in great arcs into the falling rain.

Bolan threw himself down, pulling the body of the man he'd killed over him. He was instantly soaked with blood. He heard a man outside shouting himself hoarse in sudden rage. Then the death squad outside unleashed a fusillade of hellfire.

Rounds tore through the walls and windows of the hangar in a devastating wave of lead. Bolan hugged the ground as bullets skipped off the frame of the Humvee and ricocheted wildly. Slugs sparked off the pavement, and he felt more than one impact the body shielding him. Tracer fire lit the gloom in brilliant flashes. The sounds of weapons fire drowned out the incessant rainfall, and the racket of metal slugs piercing the structure of the Quonset hut hangar was deafening.

The barrage seemed to go on forever but stopped just as suddenly as it started. Bolan blinked the blood of the corpse out of his eyes. The air he breathed was filled with dust raised by the catastrophic disturbance. His ears rang from the assault. He shifted out from under his makeshift shield, coated in the dead man's blood, and prepared himself for what he knew had to be coming next.

Outside the faceless enemy barked a command and unleashed the dogs.

Bolan waited. If he started firing right away, he'd only expose himself to another merciless barrage. But if he didn't use the P-90, he'd be ripped to shreds.

He scrambled back from the windows, staying low to avoid being backlighted in the openings. He scrambled toward the silent hulk of the Humvee in a scuttling crouch. In seconds the dogs were through the windows.

A massive beast came at him. Its lips were twisted back in a vicious snarl and its eyes seemed to burn with demonic energy. There was no concept of mercy in the animal, only the hunger for blood. Ropes of salvia hung from its slathering jaws and the growl came from a wide chest.

Two more animals leaped into the hangar through the opposite window, then a fourth followed the pack leader in. They barreled forward, snarling and barking. Bolan turned and scooped up the double-bladed ax from the pile of tools he had left next to the Humvee's bumper.

The first dog lunged, a blur of teeth and fur in the uncertain light. Bolan swung the ax like he was splitting wood. The edge of the blade whistled down and buried itself in the spine of the animal even as it went for Bolan's throat.

A dark shadow, impossibly fast and strong, darted in from his left. Bolan twisted the ax handle and slashed it hard, like a batter swinging for the fence. The blade cut through the lunging animal's throat and blood flew outwards. The animal dropped immediately but momentum carried its heavy, limp corpse directly into Bolan.

The soldier was rocked by the force of the impact. He raised the ax and thrust it into the massive muscled chest of the third animal. The blade cracked the sternum and lodged there, slicing into the heart, but the animal's speed was incredible. It snapped for Bolan's throat as it died.

There was no chance for him to stop the final animal. It leaped over the corpses of its pack members and lunged at Bolan. He dropped the blood-smeared handle of the ax, catching the attacking beast it is moved in for his throat.

The weight of the dog drove him back, pinning him against the hard rubber of the Humvee tire. His grip sank into the loose rolls of fur at the animal's neck. He pushed back with all his strength. The snapping jaws drew closer to his unprotected face.

Bolan let go of the beast with one hand and went for the pistol grip of the submachine gun pinned between himself and the dog. The muscles of his hand and arm screamed in overworked protest as he fought.

He could smell the dog's fetid breath and the odor of its fur, as he found the P-90. His fingers closed around the trigger, and he angled the gun into the dog's belly, and pulled the trigger. The darkness of the hangar was brilliantly lit though some of the sound was muffled by the heavy weight of the animal. The armor-piercing rounds punched through the animal and the struggling, snarling beast became a heavy, limp weight crushing down on Bolan.

Ears still ringing from the blast Bolan was still able to hear the field commander outside respond to the gunfire by ordering a second round of firing. A wall of lead hit the building. The stamped metal of the Quonset hut hangar began to shred and peel back under the onslaught.

Trace fire knifed through the gloom. Bolan shoved the dead attack dog off his chest and flattened himself on the ground. Behind him the Humvee frame rang as bullets pounded into it. Bolan tried to press himself into the floor to get underneath the trajectory of the fusillade.

He scrambled forward on his belly. Reaching the corpse of the man he had used as a shield, he immediately stripped the man of his submachine gun, extra magazines, pistol, a canister-shaped stun grenade and a sheathed knife.

Bullets punched through the light skin of the hangar structure and cut through the air around his head. He could feel the falling rain as it lashed into the building through the blown-out windowpanes.

A stray round plucked at the fold of his clothes on one shoulder, and a second round glanced off the heel of his boot. He heard the sickening sounds as the corpses of animals—dog and man—were struck by the bullets.

Bolan crawled until he was pointed toward the rear of the hangar and began to make his way back toward the dubious protection of the Humvee. He could feel the air split at the passing of waves of bullets just inches above his head.

On the far side front tire, Bolan rolled into the cover and lay, gasping to regain his breath.

The firing began to die off. Bolan used the lull to situate the equipment he'd taken from the corpse. If he could survive the barrages of small-arms fire long enough, the death squad would have to assault the hangar through the choke points of the barricaded door and the small windows. He hoped to hold them off long enough that unit discipline broke down and they became too afraid to try and pull him out.

Or until they got heavier weapons and brought the hangar down on top of him.

As the last rounds of the second fusillade died out, Bolan's captured phone began to vibrate.

Bolan peeked his head out around the Humvee tire and watched the front of the hangar. He worked his left hand into his pocket and pulled out the cell phone. He used a thumb to flip it open and put it against his ear.

"Go," he said.

"I'm in the air!" Grimaldi shouted.

"How? The weather hasn't broken here," Bolan answered.

"Here either," Grimaldi agreed. "We're flying in a shitstorm. I'm trying to climb above it now, but it almost dumped me in the water as I took off the damn boat. Leave the flying to me, just worry about staying alive."

"The CO let you leave?"

"Sort of. Barb ran the number on the phone you stole. The situation has changed."

"You can't land here," Bolan warned him.

"Sarge, we've got a plane. Charlie was talking to a Recon team on the craft. They had a plane with skyhook capability."

"Skyhook?" Bolan asked.

"It's our only chance. You have to make it work!" Grimaldi shouted.

"Copy that. It won't work. We'll all be killed. I'll try to set it up as best I can," Bolan barked. "I'll call you when I'm ready. Or you call me when you're overhead."

"Roger," Grimaldi acknowledged.

Bolan snapped the cell phone closed and put it away. He wondered what was so important about Helene

Burke that Washington had decided to push the very limits of plausible deniability to get him out.

As the death squad outside began shooting again, Bolan decided it didn't matter.

11

Two figures appeared at the windows and began spraying the inside of the hangar with gunfire. Bolan rolled behind the Humvee's tire then took up a position under the belly of the big vehicle. He saw the hangar door forced open and two cylinders were thrown into the room.

The Executioner opened his mouth while sticking fingers in his ears. The stun grenades tripped, brilliant flashes followed hard by thunderous *bangs* designed to disorientate and incapacitate enemy combatants.

Bolan felt the shock of the grenade concussions rattle him to his bones. The flashes blinked through his tightly shut eyes, leaving streaks across his vision. He knew what would follow the initial flash-bangs—the assault.

He yanked the pin from his own flash-bang and let the spring kick the spoon across the concrete floor. He rolled onto his side and let the canister travel under the Humvee and across the ground toward the hangar door. He saw dark silhouettes vaulting the overturned soda machine blocking the doorway as they entered the hangar, weapons up.

Bolan turned away and hunched against the coming explosion. The detonation came a second later, repeating the flash-bang attack of the first stun grenades. Bolan rolled over and scythed the muzzle of his stolen submachine gun back and forth.

The armor-piercing rounds lanced out in a loose zigzag-pattern and caught three reeling men in civilian clothes and balaclavas. They jerked and danced as the rounds tore into them, falling to the ground. Bolan shifted smoothly and caught another gunman pulling over watch in the right window. His 3-round burst struck the man and knocked him away.

Bolan turned to fire on a second gunmen in the left window, but the man jumped back to safety before the solider could gun him down. He dropped the magazine out of the P-90's well and slammed home a fresh one. His ears were ringing, and slivers and bars of light from the vehicles outside cut through the hanging smoke and dust in the hangar to illuminate in an eerie, almost ghostly fashion.

Bolan crawled from around the cover of the Humvee and scrambled on his hands and knees across the floor toward the front of the building. He angled his approach in the protective lee of the heavy soda machine and sidled up to it.

Rounds struck the machine with regularity, but the

obstacle was thick enough to absorb or deflect them. Bolan lifted up quickly and sprayed gunfire over the top of the machine, aiming his weapon toward the front of the vehicles parked like a fortress wall outside.

His rounds, coming from hasty fire, sprayed out in irregular patterns and he was rewarded with more than one exploding headlight for his efforts. He threw himself down as the death squad outside returned fire.

Bolan knew the hangar was a trap as much as a defense. The limited approaches offered by the windows and blockaded doors allowed a single gunman to control egress and thus gave Bolan a fighting chance against the greater numbers. However the thin metal walls did little to stop the incoming rounds and a lot to obscure his vision of the movements of his attackers, making a counterassault almost impossible.

He was forced to fight on the defensive to surrender momentum and initiative to the men outside with their superior firepower and greater freedom of movement. He had to make each shot count.

Some of the firing began to peter off and Bolan risked a quick look. He saw running forms falling back from peripheral positions behind the center vehicle, and he instinctively knew what was happening next.

He scrambled back toward the dubious safety of the Humvee in the center of the hangar and angled his coverage through the window to the right of the hangar door. As if on cue, two vehicles began to pull forward from the initial skirmish line formed by the phalanx of light skinned automobiles.

The death squad was attempting a full-frontal assault in order to wear him down by sheer force of numbers and superior firepower. It was no time for half measures or holding things back, Bolan decided coolly.

He reached for the pile of equipment he had dumped out of his pack and had stored behind the rear tire of the Humvee. He moved quickly, his fingers moving with practiced precision as the gun-trucks moved inexorably forward. Gunfire streaked around him as men in the beds of the pickups fired across the roof of the cabs, pouring concentrated streams of tracer fire and flying lead into the opening above his makeshift barricade.

Bolan primed his final supply of plastic explosive. He risked a look around the rear wheel well of the riddled Humvee and saw the dented, bullet scarred grille of a white Toyota pickup ram straight into the hangar door, knocking the overturned soda machine aside with a screeching impact.

The truck came to a stop under the impact, and the heavy old-fashioned soda machine skidded across the floor in a shower of sparks. The soldiers standing in the back of the pickup were thrown hard against the cab, and for a moment their deadly firing was subdued.

Bolan hurled the satchel with both hands. The compact package seemed to float through the air, then reached the pinnacle of its arc and suddenly plummeted downward.

He saw it strike the ground between the still sliding soda machine and the stalled truck. It didn't bounce but instead landed flat and rolled over once toward the front of the building. He threw himself back behind the Humvee tire and felt the vehicle rock under the impact of the sliding soda machine.

A heartbeat later the satchel charge exploded.

A rolling column of flame followed hard by thick, black smoke rushed past Bolan, clouding him with heat and choking vapors. The roar of the first explosion was followed hard by the pickup truck's gas tank detonating.

Despite the stunning, concussive force of the blast, Bolan forced himself up. He could see nothing in the bank of gray-black fog. He turned his weapon toward the burning beacon of the flaming truck engine and sprayed out a sloppy figure-eight pattern.

He choked for air in the smoke, and then suddenly cool moisture began to hammer into him. The smoke broke in a swirling moment, and he realized that his charge and the burning truck and blown out a section of the hangar front and roof.

A gunman stumbled past in the chaos, his hands pressed against bleeding ears, and put him down with a tight burst to the head. Bolan immediately dropped to his belly and stitched a second line of bullets into the smoke to knock down any other attackers. He squinted against the chemical sting of the smoke, seeing bodies and body parts strewed among the debris. Flames leaped and danced from the Toyota truck frame. His ears popped suddenly, and he could hear again in a rush.

Almost unbelievably the phone in his shirt pocket began to vibrate. He pulled it out, keeping a one-handed hold on the submachine gun's pistol grip.

"Jack!" he shouted.

"I see you burning down the jungle!" Grimaldi replied.

"I put a hole in the roof, but you'll have to come down close if you plan to make the shot." Bolan's voice was raspy.

"Copy. How many tangos left?"

Automatic-weapon fire struck the frame of the Humvee.

"Too many!" Bolan answered.

"Copy. Get down, then. I've got a surprise for them, but I'll have to drop it danger close."

"Danger close," Bolan acknowledged.

He looked toward the sky and saw that the pitch-black of the night had leeched out to a morning gray through the heavy cloud cover. Rain still fell steadily and was working to dampen the flames and beat down the smoke.

Bolan began to fire in an effort to keep the death squad back, harassing in some instances and deadly accurate in others. After the explosion and resulting devastation of his death trap the aggression had been knocked from the shooters.

He didn't hear the engines of Grimaldi's plane until the aircraft was almost on top of him. He caught a view of the silhouette flying in at treetop level. Crisscrossing arcs of tracer fire rose to meet the incoming plane.

Smoke obscured his eyes and he blinked the sting away. When he opened them again, he saw a fifty-five-gallon drum tumbling from an open door at the back of the banking plane. He caught a glimpse of Charlie Mott in brown leather jacket and yellow baseball cap in the opening, then he saw only the belly of the turning plane. He threw himself down.

He didn't see the tumbling barrel hit, but he felt the impact in a rushing wall of heat that dwarfed the explosion of his satchel charge. Jellied gasoline erupted across the ground in front of the old hangar, raising a wall of heat and flame that ignited two other vehicles in sudden bursts. Bolan saw men running like human torches in several directions as he lifted his head.

He knew what was coming next, how tight the margin of error would be, and he did his best to exploit the precious moments Grimaldi and Mott's maneuver had given him. He pulled himself up and sprinted toward the door to the tiny bathroom where he had secured Sukarnoputri.

His heart rose in his throat as he approached the door. The wooden frame had been ripped apart by gunfire. It was so riddled he could see holes the size of baseballs. His earth-filled backpack, which had served as a make-shift bulwark, had been torn apart by the intense fire. Loose dirt spilled out across the floor.

He ran up to the door and pulled the backpack out of the way. He opened the door and looked inside. Sukarnoputri lay where he had left her, blood soaked through her bandages. He knelt beside her head and his fingers found her throat.

Her flesh was cold and clammy to the touch. At last he found a weak pulse, thready and faint but present. He lifted the wounded woman into his arms.

He turned and jogged back to the Humvee. He cocked his head as he settled the woman down, hearing it then, the sound of Grimaldi bringing the plane around for another run. He lifted his submachine gun and ran out toward the twisted and burning frame of the truck used to ram the hangar door.

He could see the sky clearly, though the falling rain made it appear washed out and indistinct. He knelt by the still smoking fender and kept one eye cocked toward the gunmen separated from him by a wall of burning fuel.

The concrete was hard under his knee. The frame of the truck radiated heat like an open stove. His shirt was soaked by the falling rain, and he could smell the sickly sweet stench of scorched human flesh. Black smoke hugged the muddy ground, and blood was splattered everywhere.

Suddenly the sound of aircraft engines roared loud over head and Bolan saw the nose of Grimaldi's plane, barely fifty feet above the ground, cut out of the rain and smoke. There was a long moment as the plane cut across the top of the damaged building, and it appeared to Bolan's adrenaline amped senses in hyper-detail.

Charlie Mott appeared in the open rear hatch, and Bolan was close enough to see the look of intense concentration on the man's face. Their gazes locked across the scant distance separating them. Mott nodded once and lifted a package to his chest.

A tracer round burned the air in front of Mott and he flinched, then he heaved the box out of the aircraft and down through the hole in the hangar roof. It plummeted toward the ground as the plane zoomed out of sight.

The package dropped like a stone and came so close to where Bolan was standing that he had to jump back to dodge it. It landed hard at his feet.

Bolan wasted no time dragging the weighted package to the Humvee, where he had placed Sukarnoputri. He hauled a dull green canister out of the package and set it up right before her. A limp rubber balloon dangled from the nozzle of the helium canister. Bolan quickly pulled coils of high grade tether from the package he had opened until he had finally pulled out a harness suit.

Moving closer to Sukarnoputri he turned toward the front of the building where it opened on the burning area between the battered chain-link fence. A line of gunman scrambled up out of the smoke, slow and clumsy and unstoppable. The first one tripped hard on the lip of the hangar floor and fell. As he struggled to rise, a second one emerged behind him.

Bolan struggled to get the rig suit around Sukarnoputri. He locked the last carabineer into place and watched as still more gunmen spilled out of the cloying smoke.

He twisted the nozzle on the helium canister, quickly filling the good-sized balloon. The balloon sealed itself and popped free from the nozzle once the canister was empty. It began to rise, pulling the tether and a thousand feet of rope after it.

It bobbed against the torn lip of the hangar roof for one long moment, then slipped through the opening and rose into the sky. Bolan picked up his gun up and began firing at the approaching death squad gunners. Two of them fell back between a break in the pools of fire outside the hangar while the third dropped dead into a burning puddle of gasoline.

Bolan removed the emergency transmitter beacon from the vest pouch and placed it on the ground between his feet. He pulled his P-90 around and picked it up by the pistol grip.

Like better plans, the theory behind the skyhook was simple. Grimaldi's plane would home in on his transmitter signal, using it to vector in overhead while flying at roughly 130 knots. A Y-attachment built into the nose of the plane would catch the tether below the balloon and shunt it onto a winch operating out of either a tail ramp or belly cargo door. The winch would then reel the rope, dragging the cargo along with it.

Bolan lifted the submachine gun and sighted down

the barrel. It cracked and kicked in his hand. Thirty yards out a spray of mud kicked up just to the right of an approaching gunman in the lead of a fire team. Bolan shifted the submachine gun smoothly, gently took up the slack and squeezed the trigger.

The weapon jumped again, and this time it was black blood instead of dirt that was kicked up. The round struck the running death squad gunner in his knee, shattering the patella and tripping the man to the ground. Behind him five more gunmen charged forward. The wounded combatant fought to regain his feet.

Behind Bolan the rope uncoiled quickly, the friction causing a dry whizzing sound. He shifted and blew out the wounded man's other knee. The Indonesian went down, tried to rise and went down again. He began to crawl toward Bolan.

Bullets cut through the air around the Executioner as he hunched over Sukarnoputri's inert form. He slid his arm up tight against her body in the web strapping and lodged it securely against what he knew was coming. He felt the powerful jerk as the rope payed out and he went to one knee so the pull of the high altitude balloon would not unbalance him.

The gunmen kept coming. Bolan reset his aim and fired the submachine gun again. He was tired and the shot again pulled wide. He tried to blank everything but the mechanics of marksmanship from his mind. Each round had to count; extra ammunition was a luxury he did not have.

Suddenly he was brutally upended and dragged across the floor toward the front of the hangar. He kicked out and managed to clear the end of the Humvee as he and Sukarnoputri were lifted off the ground. The skyhook had never been intended for such close quarters. As Bolan was dragged toward the ruined front of the hangar, more Indonesian gunmen scrambled to get at him.

The gun cracked in his hand. His rounds slapped into ambulatory flesh, slowing the advance but not stopping it. His last round fired with the same sharp crack, catching an advancing killer in the thigh some twenty yards out.

The Executioner fumbled, one-handed to change magazines, but as he slid toward the hangar door a man rushed in and he lanced him in the throat with the sub-machine barrel.

He used his own momentum and the fulcrum in the man's throat to throw the killer to one side. The weight of the tumbling body tore his weapon free of his hand. He drew his fighting knife. The tether hit the sharp edge of the wall and began to run up along it. Bolan was thrown against the open hangar door and dragged up the flat surface as more death squad shooters poured in.

A combatant rushed him, and he grasped the knife and thrust his arm forward at the same time, catching the balaclava-covered face squarely, meeting force with equal force. The gunmen's features caved under the impact, and he was knocked the ground. The Indonesian immediately tried to rise.

Bolan twisted to the side as another gunman lunged toward him. Still holding fast to Sukarnoputri's webbing, he slammed his foot into the Indonesian's shoulder sending him tumbling. He tried to turn to catch the first man as he lifted up but was too slow.

The man slammed into Bolan, arms coming up to bear hug the big American around the waist. Bolan grabbed the guy's and wrenched the head hard. The Indonesian reflexively let go.

Death squad members swarmed over Bolan, and he struck out again and again, lashing with fist and elbow to shake the predators loose as he continued to rise.

The slack in the tether suddenly went tight and Bolan was pulled up hard. Unprepared, the Indonesians were sent tumbling end over end. Fifteen feet into the air the last one held on around Bolan's waist with single-minded purpose.

12

The Executioner rained blows on the killer's upturned face, fearful that the extra weight might harm the calibration of the winch in the plane a thousand feet above him. He bucked and twisted, but the man clung on with unreasonable rage.

Bolan looked up and could see the plane flying above him. Momentum had swung him out behind the specially modified transport, and he could feel the pull of the winch motor as it struggled to haul them closer to the airplane.

Grabbing one of the Indonesian hands, he systematically began to snap the fingers, one by one. The Indonesian buried his face in Bolan's leg and sunk his teeth into his thigh.

With sudden intuition Bolan realized that only drugs could explain this single-minded ferocity. He was fighting a crazed animal, not a human being. He suddenly remembered the perfume bottle and stamps he carried in his pocket. He wondered what exactly those items contained.

He broke the man's thumb, and his grip finally failed. His arms slipped away and for one long agonizing moment clung to Bolan with only the strength of jaws.

Bolan struggled on the end of the line as he fought to shake the man free. Finally his flailing fist shattered his jaw along one side but the man seemed to feel no pain and continued to hold.

Bolan's body doubled up from the torture, and he simply pressed his hand straight down into the upturned face and pushed with all he had. The man came free and scarlet blood flowed as he fell away, a chunk of Bolan's flesh still locked between his blunt jaws.

Bolan grimaced. The wound in his leg was dirty and ragged, and the cold air tore at the open injury with vicious, almost sadistic, energy. It hurt badly, and he realized he was still bobbing at the end of the tether without rhyme or reason in a dysfunctional body surf that left him buffeted by high winds.

Bolan arched his back and looked toward the plane. He was still roughly five hundred feet away out from it. He closed his mind to wide open sky, the choking clouds, the pouring rain and the deadly promise of the earth stretched wide below him. He focused on his body, a body twisting and swaying in what felt like gale force winds as he was hauled like a net full of fish toward the door of the aircraft.

He could allow himself to think of nothing else but survival. It was an ancient mantra for him by now, and he fell into its cadence with a long-practiced ease.

He snatched the sling from his abandoned weapon and tied it in a tight knot just above his leg wound. It bit into his flesh, and the blood flow began to lessen in intensity.

He tilted his head to see the rear open ramp of the plane.

Fifty feet away Mott stood in the doorway running the winch. An olive drab safety line was hooked into the airframe behind him. When he saw Bolan looking at him, he gave him a thumbs-up. The soldier closed his eyes and held on. He didn't open them again until he felt hands secure him and guide him into the cargo hold.

He could hear the hydraulic lift of the rear ramp kick in and the brightness of the sun outside was replaced by a gloomy shade. Mott reached down with a squat folding knife and cut the straps off Bolan's shoulders.

"You made it, Striker!" he shouted. "You're going to be okay. I don't know how in Christ you did it, buddy, but you made it."

"Good," Bolan whispered, exhausted. "Now I just have to get Zamira Loebis."

THE EXECUTIONER LOOKED THROUGH the door of the medical quarters. The room was kept dark except for a single light burning at the foot of the bed. Arti Sukarnoputri lay under crisp, clean sheets and a soft blanket of dull color. She was hooked up to an IV drip with a pulse oximeter on one finger, its small internal light burning red. ECG leads were attached to her body and

Bolan could watch the green lines on the display scribble and scroll as her heart beat.

Her face was very pretty, he decided and she looked at peace. There were dark bruises along the smooth line of her jaw. He hated to wake her, but it had to be done. Time was ticking the way it always seemed to be, incessant, inexorable.

He moved forward and took her hand. It was warm to the touch and small against the rough masculinity of his own. Her bones felt as delicate as eggshells in his grip. He covered her tiny hand with his, cradling it.

"Arti," he whispered.

The woman didn't move. Her breathing remained deep and regular. In the clandestine chess match that was being played out between the U.S. government and the terror mercenary Zamira Loebis, an initial gambit had been initiated and thwarted. Bolan's assault on the hit team had been scratched. Loebis's bid to capture and torture him and his contact had also been thwarted. It was a zero sum game at the moment with only a few dozen corpses to show for Bolan's efforts. It wasn't good enough.

"Arti," he said again.

Bolan's own wounds were cleaned and sewn and bandaged. He was hurt, and to keep his head clear he'd taken only enough painkiller to prevent his wounds from slowing him down. The pain was still there, reminding him, urging him on. If Zamira Loebis thought

Bolan was going to count himself lucky to have escaped with his life, then the kingpin had vastly underestimated the Executioner.

The woman turned her head in Bolan's direction, her eyes still closed. Her eyes flittered under the lids and she moaned softly.

Her eyes came open, dull with the IV analgesics, and Bolan watched them sharpen and fight to focus. Her searching gaze found his face and locked on to it. He saw her confusion melt away from her and solidify into the understanding that she was finally safe.

"You did it," she whispered. "I'm alive." She swallowed. "Where's my baby?"

She repeated the question and struggled to sit up. Bolan eased her back against the support of the mattress. She leaned back, exhausted from her brief effort. Bolan comforted her as best he could.

"You daughter is safe," he told her. "A team from my embassy picked her up along with your mother and took them to a safehouse. When you're stronger you can speak to both of them on the phone. I've been instructed to inform you that if you wish you can enter a witness protection program. We are very grateful for all that you did."

"Yes, of course," Sukarnoputri whispered. "That would be wonderful. My daughter will go to school in America."

"I just need one thing more from you," Bolan said.

"I need you to try your best to help me one last time before you go."

"I would be dead if it weren't for you," she whispered. "Whatever you need, just ask."

"Zamira Loebis," Bolan said. "He's gone to ground, disappeared. I need you to give me a name."

She did.

BOLAN STOOD ON THE DECK of the ship. A Marine sergeant with an M-4 carbine stood watch some yards away, keeping the rest of the ship's crew and contingent away from him. Bolan stared out across the dark indigo of the ocean.

He liked the smell of the salt on the air, and he could see the brilliant lights of the Jakarta skyline. Out there in Jakarta an evil man waited. A man who had thought he had escaped the reach of the Executioner.

Bolan, despite his fatigue, planned to prove him wrong.

Jack Grimaldi walked up out of a bulkhead door and strolled over to where the soldier stood on the deck. Bolan nodded toward him, then looked back over the rail of the support ship.

"How do you feel?" Grimaldi asked.

"Fine," Bolan replied with a grimace.

Only half an hour earlier Grimaldi had been able to show Bolan a picture of the murdered State Department agent Helene Burke. The guilt coming to rest at the feet of Zamira Loebis kept compounding, like interest.

The Executioner would collect the debt.

"Good enough. This should help. The material in the bottle of perfume you found is some kind of designer drug. Those stamps were soaked in it, and the compound is permeable across skin membranes."

"Well, whatever it is," Bolan said, "it made those death squad fighters almost inhuman."

"They don't know what to call it. I don't understand half of what they were saying, but it was strong enough to make a city trip out. Turn everyone into violent paranoid schizophrenics.

"That whole mad scientist thing?" Bolan shook his head. "I think I've seen that movie too."

Grimaldi laughed voice rueful. "The old ideas are the best ideas."

"Yeah," Bolan agreed. "Like, an eye for an eye."

"You want to go in tonight?"

"I looked through the gear they have on board to support Force Recon operations. There's everything I need to turn the tables on Loebis," Bolan answered. "You up for a little low-level urban night flying?"

"Jakarta will be a piece of cake after the hangar," Grimaldi said with a grin.

"Glad to hear it. I'll go down to the armory and get suited up. We'll do a pass, make sure the guy is where he's supposed to be, then we'll do the drop."

"I'll get Charlie and we'll check the Little Bird, make sure it's ready to roll."

The two men separated, and Grimaldi tried not to worry about how much Bolan's leg wound had stiffened his stride.

13

Old City, Jakarta, had been deemed a national historic landmark by the Indonesian government some years before. That designation had done little to relieve the crushing weight of poverty and squalor that marked the labyrinth of twisting, narrow lanes and haphazardly stacked buildings.

Life was cheap in Old City, and nowhere was it cheaper in that vast slum than along the waterfront. Every manner of vice was bartered there, and violence was a common experience. The commodities of criminal enterprise flowed through the area, washing dirty money and camouflaging the activities of terror merchants among the masses of impoverished but hardworking families.

Jack Grimaldi flew the helicopter low over the ocean, racing full on toward the shoreline. Bolan looked down through the bubble windshield of the agile helicopter and watched whitecaps breaking on a dark sea.

Grimaldi cut and drifted, navigating the mass of ships and boats that dotted the ocean on his insertion into one of the busiest seaports in the world.

The plan was to dispense blood and thunder in a hell storm of retribution.

The pilot popped up to a slightly higher elevation to jump a pleasure yacht and make his final run on the waterfront industrial property of José Luis Rodriguez Zapatero, ostensibly an inspector with Indonesia's customs and immigration administration.

According to Arti Sukarnoputri, he was the man who had first threatened her in the name of Zamira Loebis. DEA and Interpol files had shown intelligence revealing a connection with the property of and the fencing of materials gained through piracy along the Strait of Malacca.

Flying low to avoid Jakarta air-traffic control, Grimaldi turned sharply left and began flying south perpendicular to the wharves and docks of the Jakarta waterfront, just beyond the reach of the floodlights and streetlights. He flew the blacked out chopper by instruments and a GPS feed that ticked off the distance as they flew.

Bolan sat next to him, prepped for a hard probe in his nightfighter black, face covered with a thick balaclava. He was armed with a .45-caliber Baby Desert Eagle and a silenced Beretta 93-R. From the shipboard armory Bolan had also taken an HK MP-5 submachine gun.

Grimaldi avoided a series of power lines and cut up an abandoned alley in the narrow space between warehouses and industrial plants. Bolan turned in his seat and put both of his feet on the helicopter skid as he prepped for his assault.

The Stony Man pilot suddenly cut left, skimming above a parked flatbed truck and hopped over a chain-link fence. He came down in a parking lot behind a three-story office building set above massive loading docks and lined with tractor-trailer rigs sitting quietly unmanned.

Grimaldi hovered and Bolan dropped the last eight feet off the skid. He hit the ground smoothly, bending at the knees to absorb the impact. He ignored the pain in his thigh and raced toward a small door made of wood covered by peeling paint and set some distance away from the loading bays.

Behind the sprinting Bolan the chopper powered up and Grimaldi disappeared quickly into the night. The soldier reached into the open pocket of his left pant leg and removed what looked like a bag of a popular brand of Indonesian snack chips. Inside was a device about the size of a cigarette pack used to boost localized electronic signals.

Without breaking stride Bolan dropped the camou-flaged booster pack among the of trash and garbage that littered the place. It was instantly lost in the scat-tered rubbish.

Still running, came up to the door, lifted the MP-5 to his shoulder and triggered a silenced burst. Instantly 9 mm

Parabellum rounds struck the commercial lock mechanism on the access door and blew it apart.

Satellite imagery and downloaded blueprints had provided the information Bolan needed about where the hinges were located and the material strength of the door structure. Bolan lifted a big boot and kicked the mutilated door open.

It swung open to reveal a long hall of gleaming linoleum floors under industrial tract lighting. Bolan's rubber soles slapped a hard rhythm as he sprinted down the corridor. He ran with a loose, easy stride that ate up the interior distances, his submachine gun held at a three-quarters port arms that left the muzzle of the silenced weapon orientated toward his front.

Bolan turned a corner and raced down the short stretch then took a left-hand turn, following off the building blueprints by memory. He cut down another hall, then opened a seemingly random door where he found stairs that he immediately ascended.

He looked up and saw a stunned Indonesian man in a grubby T-shirt and jeans descending the stairs. The young man's hair had been gelled into a carefully crafted messy look and his lower lip was pierced.

The man reached for the butt of a Beretta 92 pistol that jutted from the front of his jeans. Bolan squeezed his trigger and the HK kill box cycled through a tight pattern. A trio of bloody divots appeared over the man's heart and he tumbled.

Bolan danced past the falling corpse and raced up the stairs to the next landing. He bypassed the landing door and took the next flight of steps, running faster, two steps at a time.

He reached the top of the stairs, pulled open the door and entered a less industrial looking hallway.

The office space was sheathed in wood flooring and paneling. The lighting was soft. Pictures of shorelines, ocean views and ships were interspersed along the walls. The air was heavy with the smell of freshener and cleaning products. At the far end of the hallway two men in dark suits lounged in front of a pair of oak double doors.

Bolan ran down the hallway, a nightsuited terror hurtling straight toward the stunned men. His weapon was up and ready as he charged forward without uttering a word. The men scrambled to liberate weapons beneath suit jackets.

Bolan saw the shirts of the men puff up as the 9 mm slugs sliced into them. The gunners staggered backward under the impact of the man-killer rounds. Seeing no blood on the bulky framed bodies, Bolan realized the bodyguards were wearing vests.

While the two men shuddered under the initial impacts, Bolan shifted his weapon on the run and triggered it twice more. Each man took a 3-round burst to the head that dashed his skull open and sprayed blood and brains across the wood paneling.

The men dropped hard to the floor. Bolan raced past

them and snapped open the door leading into the inner sanctum. He felt the stitches in his leg wound pull in protest at his vigorous actions. Blood leaked down his leg, sticking the cloth of his pants to his skin.

He stepped across the threshold, holding the MP-5 one-handed as he transitioned through the entranceway. He found a reception lobby commanded by a large desk and outfitted with several comfortable chairs.

Three men lounged around the room reading magazines and smoking cigarettes. Bolan took the man directly in front of him. The guy held his P-90 in his lap while he sat on the edge of the desk and looked at a glossy magazine. Bolan's burst punched through the shiny pictures of the periodical and mangled the flesh and cartilage of the man's throat. Blood splattered across the phone, and clock and keyboard on the desk.

The Executioner came to a stop in the middle of the room. He shifted to his left. Three 9 mm bullets cracked a second gunman's head like an egg. Bolan snapped to his right, body turning like a gun turret as he brought his weapon to bear on the last man. The gunner rose, smoking cigarette tumbling away as he tried to fire his submachine gun from the hip. Fear caused him to trigger his weapon too soon, and a 3-round burst of 5.7 mm armor-piercing rounds burned into the carpet.

Bolan's burst caught him between chin and nose. The man absorbed the rounds and tumbled forward.

An inner door to the office was thrown open and a

man in an expensive business suit ran out. Bolan held his fire for a split second to identify his target, allowing the pistol wielding gunmen to get off a round.

The .40-caliber bullet flew wide, and Bolan scythed the man's feet out from under him then finished him off with a tight burst to the top of his head. The soldier angled his weapon up, then fired a burst through the doorway to keep the room's occupants down as he charged in.

Two men were seated around a desk that made the impressive table in the reception area look insubstantial by comparison. He identified Zapatero immediately. The man had thrown himself to the carpet while the second man in the room began firing a Glock 17 as soon as Bolan crossed the threshold.

The Executioner's initial burst of harassing fire had thrown the man off balance and his shot flew wild. Bolan drew down on him and put three tight bursts into his body, splashing him across the conference table and interior décor.

"Zapatero!" Bolan snarled. "Stay down and you might live."

Bolan ran forward and shoved the smoking barrel of his weapon into Zapatero's face. He pressed down hard into the crime lord's face, intimidating him. His voice was a cold wind to the helpless man.

"Don't talk, Zapatero. Don't even breathe. You do and I'll ventilate your thick skull."

Bolan patted down the corrupt official's body removing a handgun and sliding it behind his own back. He jerked the man's wallet out of a pocket and scattered the contents across the carpet. He took an expensive, sleek cell phone out and smashed it against the edge of the desk. If Zapatero wanted to make a phone call later, he would be forced to use a landline.

Bolan finished scattering the contents of Zapatero's suit pockets, and as he did so he managed to slip a tiny microphone and tracking device mounted on a slim straight pin along the lining of his jacket. Mission accomplished, Bolan struck Zapatero across the face with the muzzle of the submachine gun to further confuse and distract the man.

"It's not here, I want it," Bolan said. He wanted nothing specific from the kingpin but only used the words to distract him from his true intentions. "You tell Zamira Loebis I want it, and I'm coming for it. You tell him he should have killed me at the old hangar, and now he's going to pay for the mistake. You tell him that."

Bolan lifted his weapon and brought the butt of it down on the pinned man's head, cracking it hard into the floor. Zapatero shuddered under the impact and went limp. The terrified man fought against his sense of vertigo and tried to focus his eyes again.

When he looked up the Executioner was gone.

BOLAN RACED OUT of the building. He left the office suite and ran down the hall, the soles of his boots slick with spilled blood. He raced down the stairs, hurdled the quickly cooling corpse of his first kill and pushed back out into the hallway on the ground floor. He sprinted back out the way he had come and kicked his way clear of the access door to jog out into the parking lot.

He double-timed across the parking lot toward the back fence. Suddenly Jack Grimaldi's helicopter darted around a building and swooped down to pick him up. Bolan jogged into the rotor wash and slid into the copilot's seat.

There was a whine of engines as Grimaldi reversed his pitch and pulled away from the ground, snatching Bolan away to safety.

"How'd it go?" he asked as Bolan slipped on his flight helmet."

"Pretty smooth," Bolan allowed. "I bloodied Loebis's nose, and I'm sure Zapatero has no idea I planted that receiver-tracer on him. As long as the booster I hid in the parking lot keeps working, it went off without a hitch."

"Let's hope so," Grimaldi agreed and cut out toward the dark expanse of the ocean.

Bolan clicked off the helicopter's internal link and made a sat-com connection. "The Easter egg is in place," he told Barbara Price.

"Bear's got the signal clear as sunshine," the Stony Man mission controller said. "We have translation programs burning right now. You rattled that guy's cage pretty well, Striker."

"Glad to hear it."

"He's on the phone now. He's panicking. We're triangulating the signal now."

Bolan waited for several long moments while the Stony Man cyberwizards worked their magic.

"Keep your fingers crossed, Striker," Price said. "Zapatero is demanding to talk to Loebis. He's only got a lieutenant now. Hold on."

Grimaldi kept the chopper in the air over international waters while they waited to see if their cowboy gambit would play out or not.

After a moment Price came back on the line. "All right. It's not perfect but it is workable. Zamira Loebis is out of the country according to this lieutenant Zapatero keeps calling Raya. I'll put Carmen Delahunt on trying to match a face to the name, but it may be moot. Raya has told Zapatero to come meet with him. As long as the tracer keeps working, he should lead you right to where Raya is."

"Copy that, Barb," Bolan said. "Jack's got the signal strong. So far so good."

"Zapatero hung up. I'll get back to you if we're able to forward anything else," Price said.

"Right. In the meantime we'll shadow Zapatero," Bolan said.

"Be careful, Striker."

Bolan signed off and grinned at Grimaldi. "Let's roll."

14

Carmen Delahunt obtained a report on the Indonesian man named Raya Pancasila very quickly.

Pancasila was an intelligence officer charged with security issues involving the Indonesian Ministry of Tourism. He used his position to broker deals and move large amounts of illicit currency out of his country and into the tax havens created by the sultan of Brunei to facilitate trade and economic diversity among the nations of the South China Sea.

His partnership with the corrupt Zamira Loebis had made him a wealthy and influential man. Like Loebis he was suspected of working as a paid stringer for the intelligence agencies of Vietnam and China and in helping North Korean agents navigate the complicated banking systems of Taiwan and Kuala Lumpur.

His operation was not small-time. If pirates in the region took an entire commercial vessel and wanted to dump both cargo and ship, then Raya Pancasila was the man who could connect buyer with seller.

If anyone knew where Zamira Loebis had gone to ground, then it was Raya Pancasila. It was that simple.

Thirty minutes after Bolan's raid on the offices of José Luis Rodríguez Zapatero, the man met with Pancasila at a city park on the outskirts of Jakarta. Jack Grimaldi kept the helicopter well above and to the west of the meeting to avoid detection, but close enough for the booster pack in his communications gear to relay the signal they picked up from Zapatero's receiver-tracer back to Stony Man Farm.

Unable to see the action directly, Bolan listened intently. He heard the obviously flustered Zapatero open his car door and get out of his vehicle and call out to someone.

"He's greeting Raya," Price said. "Raya's just told him to put his hands on the hood of his car."

"They'll never find a stick-pin unit with a pat down," Grimaldi murmured.

"Damn!" Price snarled over their ear sets.

"What?" Both Grimaldi and Bolan spoke.

"They're using a wand," she said.

"Crap," Grimaldi muttered.

Bolan stayed quiet but turned the corners of his mouth down in a thin, hard line. An electronic wand of the kind someone like Raya Pancasila was likely to have access to would detect the signal put out by even a passive transmitter like the one Bolan had planted on Zapatero.

There was a clearly audible chirping through the eat

sets, then a flurry of scuffling and excited shouts. A hoarse-throated man was screaming something, enraged. There was pleading in a voice Bolan recognized as Zapatero.

Then there was a gunshot.

Then three more.

"Raya just shot Zapatero!" Price said.

"Go! Go!" Bolan yelled at Grimaldi.

The Stony Man pilot pushed his control yoke hard to the side and turned the chopper in a wide sweep. He dipped his nose and cut in toward the Indonesian shore one more time.

They had to cover the distance to the meet sight and identify Raya Pancasila's vehicle before the man left. Zapatero's corpse would leave the Stony Man crew with only a trail growing just as cold as the man's body if they didn't act quickly.

Grimaldi laid the engines wide open. The night was still dark as he raced toward the GPS coordinates indicated by Zapatero's transmitter.

Bolan's hands worked on the textured grips of his weapon. "Barb," he said into his com-link.

"Go ahead, Striker," she answered over the secure line.

"I'm going to try for an Extraordinary Rendition," he said.

The oblique phrase referred to a snatch operation in some cases and the returning of captured terrorists to their countries of record in others. What Bolan meant now was clear. He was going to try to take Raya Pancasila and make him talk.

"Copy that, Striker," Price answered. "It'll have to be a field interrogation though," she warned. "The Marine commander is not authorized for those kinds of blackside activities on his ship."

"Understood," Bolan replied.

Grimaldi continued to fly the like a bat out of hell. The helicopter overshot the park on the outskirts of Jakarta. Below them Zapatero's dark blue Mercedes sat in a paved drive. The driver's door hung open and Zapatero's corpse was easily visible beside the vehicle.

"Keep going!" Bolan shouted.

He pointed at a three-vehicle convoy speeding down a winding road toward the scenic park. The vehicles were all black Lincoln Navigators with diplomatic reflective windows. The chance of them being anyone but Raya Pancasila was beyond remote at this late hour.

Still, Bolan knew he had to be sure.

The helicopter covered the ground in a straight line, burning up the distance in the whirlwind revolutions of its rotor wash. The vehicles loomed larger as Grimaldi flew.

"Bring it around and I'll wave them off!" Bolan instructed.

Grimaldi nodded once and swung the chopper into play. Bolan knew he could not take the chance of firing on innocents. The chopper cut past the lead vehicle in the convoy, appearing out of the night like a mechanized thunderbolt.

Having alerted the convoy to his presence, Grimaldi looped out wide and cut back in again, turning so that Bolan was now exposed to the short line of expensive SUVs. The soldier kept his weapon down as he leaned out of the passenger door, one foot on the skid.

He held out his gloved hand and waved the driver down.

Nothing happened and the convoy continued to speed in the direction of the hovering helicopter. Grimaldi gently toyed with the helicopter stick and let the aircraft drift just off to the side. The blacked-out window on the passenger side of the lead Navigator powered down.

A square face, eyes covered by black glasses, appeared on a stout neck encircled by a crisp white dress shirt. The stony-faced Indonesian wore a tightly groomed beard and his hair was neat and slick.

The muzzle of the P-90 submachine gun was instantly recognizable to Bolan as it emerged over the lip of the car window in the man's thick fists. The man grinned.

"Go!" Bolan yelled.

Grimaldi cut the helicopter hard to the side and lifted up, clawing for altitude. Bolan saw the star-patterned muzzle-flash splash outward. The night cloaked the burning rounds, and none of them whistled close as Grimaldi performed his evasive maneuvers.

"I think that's Raya!" Grimaldi yelled.

"I think you're right," Bolan replied. "Bring it in tight behind the tail vehicle."

Grimaldi had already anticipated Bolan's instructions and the helicopter moved in a comma pattern, coming up behind the last vehicle.

Without hesitation Bolan swept his MP-5 up and began firing precise bursts on the luxury vehicle. To his surprise the vehicle didn't appear to be armored. Bolan's first exploratory burst flew wide and knocked sparks off the road.

He triggered another blast. A trio cascade of gleaming brass flew out of the ejection port and was snatched away by the streaming wind just outside the helicopter door.

He saw the window of the rear hatch door spiderweb then shatter. A second later the snout of a weapon appeared in the hole. From the rear driver's side door a man clambered out the window and tried to bring a P-90 submachine to bear across the roof of the SUV. Both weapons began to fire simultaneously.

Grimaldi stood the chopper on its nose, then darted to the left to dodge the attack while still providing Bolan with lines of engagement. The soldier pressed the trigger down. The weapon stuttered in his gasp as he cycled it through a series of 3-round bursts.

His bullets riddled the metal of the SUV's roof and knocked paint off the rear doors. More of his rounds skidded off the road in showers of sparks. Both he and

Grimaldi heard stray rounds from below strike the metal superstructure of the helicopter.

Grimaldi cut back in behind the vehicle, and Bolan put a 3-round burst directly through the shattered window on the rear hatch door. He caught a flash of a figure tumbling away, and then Grimaldi jerked them out of the second gunman's line of fire and up into the air.

"Christ!" Grimaldi shouted.

Bolan was almost thrown out of the helicopter as the ace pilot was forced to suddenly slip around a row of telephone poles and power lines. The veteran pilot cut it close, just inching his skids above the danger, but once he was clear of the surprise obstacle he brought the bird back around for the attack.

Bolan settled in and began firing his weapon in earnest. The bullets climbed the side of the vehicle in visible dimples until the submachine gunner hanging out the window was riddled.

The man dropped his weapon from limp fingers and it fell to the ground. It bounced off the road as the gunner followed his weapon. He slipped over the edge of the car door and dangled for a moment before being sucked under the tires.

The vehicle lurched to the side as it bumped over the body, and Grimaldi swung immediately into action with a impeccably timed movement. The pilot cut between the second and third vehicles right in front of the trailing car. Bolan ignored the man firing at him from the front passenger window just as Grimaldi forced himself to ignore the danger coming from rear-facing shooters in the middle vehicle.

Bolan coolly sprayed the engine compartment of the last Navigator. He pumped triple hammer burst after triple hammer burst into the vehicle. The hood was transformed into a sieve, and after a moment both steam and smoke began to billow out from under the hood.

After a wild moment the clasp on the front of the hood was sheared off by a subsonic 9 mm round and it snapped open. The violent wind stream instantly flipped the hood open, obscuring the driver's view. The Lincoln Navigator suddenly shot off the road out of control as Grimaldi was forced to pull the helicopter out of the way of renewed streams of fire coming from the second vehicle.

Bullets punched holes into the shatterproof and reinforced windshield of the agile helicopter. Grimaldi popped up to an altitude of several hundred feet and banked out of range of the small-arms fire pouring from the convoy.

Bolan watched the last vehicle as it careened out of control across the grass and smashed into a park bench under a streetlight. The lead vehicle was reaching the end of the access road for touring the park where it joined a major thoroughfare.

"All right," Grimaldi said. "We know Raya wasn't in the tail vehicle!"

"Either that or he needs to hire more dedicated bodyguards," Bolan allowed.

From his elevated vantage point, Bolan could see that the upcoming road was empty of traffic. He had been given a break, and he intended to exploit it to the fullest.

"Let's knock him off the road before they make it to more populated areas," Bolan urged.

Grimaldi was already pushing the helicopter down toward the fleeing automobiles. The major road ran downhill through tropical forest carefully cultivated back from the two lane highway. The racing SUVs straddled the center lane to command more maneuverability on the road.

Gun muzzles jutted from the windows of the vehicles as the occupants prepared for another attack by the helicopter. Bolan knew time was of the essence. A man with Pancasila's connections would not hesitate to utilize them in bringing help from official police sources. The matter of Zapatero's corpse would be a mere triviality to be swept under the rug. Bolan would not draw down on honest policemen merely attempting to enforce the laws of their nation. If he was going to take Raya Pancasila, he needed to do so immediately.

"We'll take the first vehicle," Bolan said. "Maybe force the second to stall."

"Copy," Grimaldi answered through gritted teeth as he fought into position.

Bolan leaned out as Grimaldi flew past the convoy, then doubled quickly back to race at them. He used his sling like a second hand as he jammed the folding stock of his MP-5 into his shoulder and steadied the weapon by the pistol grip. With his left hand he steadied himself.

From below shooters began to converge on the charging helicopter. Bolan eased his breath out through his nostrils and pinched the trigger back. The weapon bucked. He ceased fire and reorientated his weapon, then depressed the trigger again. He repeated the process a third time as Grimaldi descended upon the speeding SUVs.

Bullets streaked past the helicopter on both sides. The windshield took several more hits, and the undercarriage of the helicopter whined in protest at ricochets and small-caliber rounds being deflected. Bolan ignored it all. With cool detachment and a sniper's deadly skill, he worked his black magic on his enemies.

His rounds punched into the deeply tinted windshield of the leading Lincoln Navigator. They clawed through the safety glass and bored out softball-sized craters. Bolan put his next burst just next to the first and the entire windshield collapsed in an avalanche of flying glass, most of which was swept back into the vehicle cab by the wind.

The driver had iron nerves. He fought to control the speeding behemoth of a vehicle even as he tried to shield his face with one arm. His efforts were futile as Bolan put a bullet in his sternum. The man was pinned back against the white leather of his seat, both hands flying from the wheel.

The vehicle began to drift immediately without a driver's hand to steady it. The man sitting in the passenger seat lunged for the wheel as Grimaldi flew the helicopter directly toward them just feet above the road, using the lead vehicle's own bulk to shield them from fire originating in the second SUV.

Bolan neatly placed another 3-round burst into the passenger just as the man's frantic fingers found the wheel. His bullets struck the bodyguard under his stretched-out arm, caving in ribs and shredding heart and lungs for an instant kill. The man's desperate reach turned into a death grip that the pulled the speeding vehicle's steering wheel in the opposite direction of its headlong drift.

The vehicle began to overcorrect as Grimaldi pulled up at the last minute, throwing Bolan back into his seat. The skids cleared the turning SUV by inches as it showed its belly to the second vehicle.

The helicopter as the submachine gunners in Pancisila's vehicle opened fire. Bullets punched through the helicopter's floor and were soaked up by the Kevlar flooring placed there. Each round made a sound like solid punch connecting on a heavy bag.

A stray bullet cracked into the windshield, opening a coin-sized hole in the reinforced safety glass. Then the Stony Man pilot took them momentarily out of danger.

The out of control vehicle overcorrected and suddenly popped up on two wheels, skidding almost perpendicular to the road before flipping and rolling. As Grimaldi spun the helicopter around, Bolan twisted against the centrifugal force to witness the events below.

The second vehicle rushed headlong into the tumbling SUV, T-boning it with a crash so hard Bolan could hear it clearly up in the helicopter. The gas tank secured on the vehicle undercarriage split open under the impact and even with only the intermittent illumination of streetlights Bolan could see the volatile fluid gushing out and spreading across the road in a dark stain.

The SUV went into a slide and the friction between asphalt and metal caused pinwheels of sparks. The spilled gasoline lit immediately, and a wall of flame erupted around the overturned vehicle.

The driver of the final operable SUV was forced to jam on the brakes as a sheet of flame briefly engulfed the front of his vehicle. Bolan knew that action had to be throwing the occupants forward and bouncing them around the inside of the cab. The vehicle slammed to a stop.

"Now! Now!" Bolan shouted.

Grimaldi swung alongside the Navigator and the Executioner brought his guns to bear.

As the Stony Man pilot brought the helicopter down even with the stalled SUV, Bolan let his submachine gun dangle from its sling off his torso. With smooth movement his right hand found the butt of his Desert Eagle.

He drew the hand cannon and leveled it as they zipped past the stalled vehicle. Through powered-down windows Bolan could see the passengers bouncing off the seats, trying to escape the assault.

The big gun boomed three times.

The first slug shattered the driver's-side window from less than ten feet away. The bullet struck the driver hard in the side of the head and Bolan saw blood and brain matter spraying out to saturate the Indonesian bodyguard sitting the passenger seat.

The next two rounds chewed through the Lincoln Navigator's engine block, instantly rendering the vehicle inoperable. Grimaldi climbed sharply up and spun the chopper on its nose in order to make another pass.

As the helicopter turned, the combatants spilled from the now useless vehicle and began scrambling toward the tree line. Bolan saw a tall, almost cadaverously thin individual being helped by two shorter, stockier men holding P-90 submachine guns in their free hands. After those three only one other man emerged from the stalled vehicle.

Bolan leveled the Desert Eagle and squeezed the trigger as the man turned and opened fire with his submachine gun, the big .45 round striking the gunner center mass and carving a gouge as big as a cereal bowl out of his side. The man was knocked to the ground where a creeping finger of burning gasoline immediately set his hair on fire.

"Here we go!" Grimaldi shouted.

The running men realized they would never reach the dubious sanctuary of the wood line in time. The remaining bodyguards turned in defense of their boss. One threw Pancasila down to the ground and hunched over him as he lifted his submachine gun.

The second paramilitary operator turned in the road and pressed the stock of his weapon to his shoulder. Bolan could see this was the man who had been splashed so liberally with his teammate's blood. His suit was stained with the sticky residue of the driver's death. Both men fired their weapons as Grimaldi swept down on them in the helicopter.

The range was dangerously close. More bullets opened jagged holes in the windshield of the helicopter. Bolan shot the first man with his Desert Eagle.

The player was knocked to the ground with merciless force. Bolan shifted his aim and eased back on the trigger of the .45 Magnum handgun once more. In a splash of crimson the last bodyguard lost his right arm at the elbow and fell to the ground in shock.

Grimaldi saw the situation and reacted immediately. He flared into a hard hover and dropped straight down toward the ground. At eight feet Bolan simply leaped clear of the hovering aircraft and onto the road. He dropped like a stone, landing on widespread feet and bending sharply at the knees to compensate for the impact.

The stitches in his legs snapped like guitar strings in protest and what had been a slow leak became a spurting gush of blood from the ragged bite wound. He winced in pain but his hand was steady on his gun as he saw

Raya Pancasila lunge toward his shell-shocked body-guard's weapon.

The Desert Eagle roared in Bolan's fist. The round struck the submachine gun and shattered the receiver and forestock into a dozen pieces. Pancasila snatched his hand back from the ruined weapon and shoved bruised fingers into his mouth like a petulant child.

Bolan shifted his aim to cover the wounded body-guard in time to see the man slump fully to the ground. The man laid his head down on the warm pavement and went to sleep forever.

Bolan turned and looked at the huddled Raya Pancasila. Behind him Grimaldi settled the agile helicopter onto the road. To his side the wreck of the SUV blazed like a bonfire, casting wild, weird shadows across the scene.

In the flickering light Bolan stepped forward. He loomed large over the Indonesian criminal.

The Executioner's voice was gravel on a tombstone as he spoke.

"Mr. Pancasila. I've been wanting to ask you a few questions."

15

The sampan sat at the end of its tether, bobbing in the slow, warm current of the Brunei River. No lights showed from the craft, which was traditional in structure with a thatch roofed covering the center. It was unremarkable among the considerable river traffic, just another transport or fishing boat among hundreds on the muddy brown river.

Charlie Mott sat in the bow of the flat-bottomed craft. He smoked in a casual manner and watched the river traffic with lazy indifference. Under a burlap sack next to his feet was a well-oiled AK-104, Kalashnikov carbine. The weapon was loaded with a 30-round banana clip and a second magazine had been taped, upside down, to the first to facilitate speedy reloading under fire should the need arise.

At the back of the vessel a crude wooden hatch had been constructed around the outboard motor. The wood was dull from age and soft from sea spray and river water. Inside the haphazard looking construct were twin

200-horsepower engines capable of propelling the boat along at more than 60 knots. The pedestrian looking sampan could out perform anything on the river except for the Royal Brunei navy's fast patrol boats.

Out on the north shore of the river, the lights of Kampong Ayer illuminated the urban enclave among the mangrove swamps. Kampong Ayer, the water village as it was called, consisted of thirty thousand residents situated among three thousand structures on thirty-six miles of boardwalks. The entire Kampong Ayer suburb of Bandar Seri Begawan—the capital of Brunei—extended over the water on stilts. The numerous mosques, restaurants, shops and homes formed around bridges and canals like a version of Venice.

Inside the cover of the sampan's shelter the Executioner readied himself. He reached over one shoulder and grabbed a neoprene lead attached to the zipper on the back of his matte black wet suit and pulled it closed. He slung an Ingram M-11 equipped with sound suppressor across his body, muzzle down.

Bolan sweated freely in the wet suit as he secured a diver knife to his calf and then slid on swim fins. The inside of the sampan shelter held no light, allowing his vision to acclimate to the darkness.

He felt the gentle pull and sway of the current rocking the flat bottom of the sampan as he reached over and opened the diver hatch built into the vessel's hull. Immediately the cramped quarters of the little thatch-roofed shelter filled with the stench of the dirty water. Bolan leaned back and slipped in the mouthpiece of the closed-circuit diving kit he wore.

He tested the apparatus, then checked the luminous readout on his dive watch. Strapped to his dive vest were several prepared Semtex shaped charges. The muted sound of air passing through his rebreather echoed in his ears as he readied himself and the underwater navigational device that would guide him to his target.

When he was at last satisfied, he slid smoothly through the open hatch and into the dark water. Instantly Bolan was enveloped by another world. Carefully adjusting his buoyancy as the current pushed him clear of the sampan, he checked his compass and orientated himself correctly. He pushed off into the dense black with powerful sweeps of his dive fins.

He started his approach well upriver from his target and he swam at a sharp angle toward it, using the current to speed his movement and conserve energy. Once he was well clear of the sampan the support asset, an Indonesian operative named Ling Cao, would move the flat-bottomed boat into position downriver from the target toward the mouth of Brunei Bay.

The moonscape of the river bottom began to appear in murky patches. Bolan kept a sharp look on his watch to gauge the passage of time because the silent, dark world he swam through obscured his natural senses.

Kicking free of the stronger currents moving through the center of the river, Bolan headed to the shore.

He was forced to slow himself to avoid becoming entangled in the forest of anchor tether lines from the multitude of boats secured around Kampong Ayer. Bolan was forced to slow even further as anchor chains and ropes gave way to a labyrinth of support beams and pylons under the bustling homes and boardwalks of the waterside village.

The water grew murkier and more clouded as Bolan entered the built-up urban area. Lights from the structures above illuminated pockets and pools of the river. Fish darted in and out around the swimmer. The Brunei River was home to more than five hundred species of fish, including twelve types of shrimp. But Bolan knew the most dangerous creatures in the river, other than men, were crocodiles. They tended to eschew the more populated areas for the mangrove swamps. Bolan hoped that would prove true for the venomous coral and sea snakes that sometimes found their way downriver from Brunei Bay.

Passing over the ruins of an old rowboat rotting at the bottom of the river, Bolan swam up against a slimy wooden pillar and double checked his instruments. Slowly he drew his feet below him and allowed his buoyancy to adjust until he was resting against the beam near the bottom of the river.

With economy of motion, Bolan began to breakout

and place his underwater demolitions packets, fitting each charge with a timing pencil. Before activating the devices Bolan would visually double-check that his target was correct and that collateral damage would not be a factor. The Executioner had always waged his war in eternal vigilance against the death of innocents caught in the cross-fire.

After finishing preparations on the last charge, Bolan kicked his way slowly toward the surface. His target this night was a timeless scourge that had emerged with a new face in recent decades.

Pirates.

Bolan kicked smoothly toward a support beam. He came up against the stilt and gathered his energy. He bobbed once in the water, then kicked himself up hard to a joist crevice.

His fingers found the edge, and he jammed his hand into the opening. He made a fist, locking himself into the hole, and used the anchor point to pull himself upward. His other hand came up and grasped the edge. Slick with river water he locked his legs tight against the beam and strained every muscle to inch up the unforgiving surface.

He kicked into position, then adjusted his grip. Using both hands now, he drew up his legs and wrapped them around the angled joist pole. He struggled into position until he was balanced.

Looking out through the tangle of beams and cross supports toward where a gangplank ran down to a dock adjacent to the house, he saw a pair of men in light-weight clothes standing at the edge of the platform. Beyond them several high-end watercraft were secured by mooring lines.

Bolan watched the men talking, their voices murmurs on the night air. They smoked cigarettes and paced in a restless manner. After a moment one of the men scratched underneath his open short-sleeve shirt and Bolan saw the butt of a pistol tucked in his waistband at the small of his back.

Making sure he was unobserved by the sentries, Bolan continued with his infiltration.

He slid in among the maze of wooden support beams and rafterlike arches that ran under the large building. He clambered over a beam and inched his way toward the back of the pagodalike dwelling. He heard a familiar squeaking and snapped his head around.

A fat gray rat sat watching him from several beams over. The beady eyes reflected light and rat's long, scaly tail dangled down, providing balance. The big rodent drew back fur-covered lips, revealing crooked sharp teeth. It hissed like a cat. Behind it Bolan could see more rats running along the beams.

The soldier reached out with his left arm and pushed it against a crossbeam for support. He grabbed another one just above his head in an underhand grip and pulled himself through a narrow cross section of interlocking timbers.

The wood was slick with moisture. The entire bottom of the house smelled like damp rot. He felt a strange sensation move across the back of his braced hand and he looked over quickly. A centipede almost fourteen inches long scurried out of the shadows, trampled across Bolan's exposed flesh and disappeared over the edge of the beam.

Bolan drew up his legs and sat on his haunches as he struggled into position. Directly above his head he heard the sound of footsteps. The floorboards creaked in protest, and he remained motionless as the person overhead crossed the room he was below. Once the footsteps had retreated he reached out, grasped a support beam like a child playing on playground monkey bars and swung out into space. He hung for a moment, twelve feet above the sluggishly moving current close in against the shore.

He swung for a moment, rocking back and forth to gather momentum, then let go with one hand and reached for another beam. He grasped it, then moved his other hand toward the beam. The strain ran up through the muscles of his back into his shoulders and tensed arms to where his forearms knotted under the strain.

Bolan adjusted his grip and began walking his body down the beam going hand-over-hand. Once he got close to a beam near the outside of the structure, he lifted his legs and snaked around the joist support. He slid into position and forced himself into the space.

He adjusted the M-11 until it was secured tightly against his body on its sling. He flexed his hands several times, forcing blood into them to increase their limberness, and then he swung into action for his final approach.

Reached out from under the house and found a finger hold, he tested his grip, then carefully suspended himself, holding on with just one hand. He moved slowly to avoid overextending himself.

He carefully reached up with his other hand and slid it into place next to the first, slowly pulling himself up into position.

The Executioner slid over the edge of the ornate railing and crouched on the spacious deck overlooking the water. He grabbed his weapon and released it for quick use. He quickly crossed the deck to where a single light burned with a subdued yellow glare, dozens of insects fluttering around it.

He unscrewed the lightbulb, plunging the balcony into darkness, then waited tensed. No cry of alarm rang out. A few vessels moved slowly out on the river, and he could see scattered groups of pedestrians moving along the spokes of connected boardwalks. Their laughter came faintly to his ears as did the sound of a passenger jet flying overhead.

The breeze was stronger here than under the house, and it brought the smell of flowers and cigarette smoke and the river to his nose. From inside the dark house Bolan could hear nothing.

The Executioner set his earpiece into place and spoke into it.

"I'm in," he whispered.

Bolan moved to the sliding glass doors leading into the house and gently pulled on the handle.

It was locked.

He knelt by the door, using the patio's furniture to camouflage his shape, pulled a lock-pick gun from a pouch and inserted the prongs into the commercial lock. He squeezed the lever and pried the bolt mechanism into the open position.

He put the lock-pick device away and then reached up and slid the door open. It slid along smoothly on its grooved track, but the noise sounded deafening to his keyed-up senses.

He stepped through the opening and into the house.

16

The Executioner stepped across the threshold and moved immediately to his right, putting his back against the wall and negating his silhouette. The room was dark, but now that he was inside the house he could hear the murmur of voices from other rooms and the sounds of people moving about.

He looked around and saw several incense sticks burning on shelves and a countertop. A vase had been filled with freshly cut orchids.

According to Raya Pancasila, the meeting between the disparate groups had been arranged as a leader-only event. Each representative was allowed only one bodyguard. Bolan had felt grimly satisfied when Pancasila had confirmed it had been the Executioner's own activities that had led to the emergency summit.

Bolan scanned the room. Furniture was scattered around and a mounted television took up the position of focus on one wall of the long, narrow room. He began weaving around couches and chairs as he made his way toward a door in the far wall.

A bar of light shone underneath it.

Upon reaching the door by halted, touching the wood lightly with the fingers of his left hand. He turned his head and listened, the silenced M-11 held at the ready. He could hear a conversation coming from the other side of the door.

He frowned. Pancasila's description of the house had been precise and so far accurate in every detail. The door to the television room should open to a short hallway directly across from a door to a shower and bathroom. If Bolan turned left, he would be led out into the front of the house where the living room, sun room, kitchen and dining areas were.

If he turned right, he would find a circular metal staircase leading to the suites on the second floor of the stilt house. He supposed someone could be using the bathroom, but it seemed odd that people would be having a conversation in the hallway unless they were posted guards.

He heard laughter from outside the door.

Bolan eased to the side and put his back to the wall next to the door. He reached out his left arm and curled his fingers around the doorknob. He raised the M-11 machine pistol and held it ready across his body. Slowly he turned the knob until he heard the faintest click of the latch receding into the lock housing.

Gently he eased open the door a crack and peered out. A sliver of yellow light spilled in through the opening and crossed Bolan's face. Behind him his footprints were damp on the hardwood floor.

Out in the hallway he saw two men. Both had goatees and tattoos visible on their necks. They were laughing and talking. Like the men on the dock, they wore short-sleeve button-down shirts over white tank tops. Bolan could see the shoulder holster housing the Beretta 92 pistol under one man's arm beneath the shirt. The other man was holding a submachine gun loosely in his left hand.

Behind them a twisting, circular staircase narrow enough to permit only one person at a time rose up through an opening in the low ceiling toward the second floor of the house.

The shorter man suddenly stood straighter. Still laughing his gaze fell across the slightly open door. The smile dropped from the man's face like a stone plummeting down a well.

Bolan used his left hand to swing the door wide. In his right hand the silenced Ingram M-11 jumped and bucked in his grip. Spinning spent shell casings arced out and rained down around Bolan's feet.

The submachine-gun wielding sentry took the rounds in the side of his shoulder, neck and face as he turned to see what was happening.

His blood flew across the wall and splattered his partner across the face as he fell. The first sentry looked stunned as gore from his fellow gunman slapped into him. His hand faltered as he reached for his holstered pistol.

Bolan's burst struck him in a tight fastball that staggered him backward. The man bumped off the wall and turned in a slow half-circle to collapse on top of his partner.

Bolan sprang into motion. Moving out of the room he quickly dragged the bloody corpses into the room. They left smears of crimson in the hall behind them and the wall was speckled with their blood, but there was no time to repair an impossible situation.

Bolan closed the door behind him and approached the stairs. He could hear the sound of a stereo or television coming from behind him, as well as voices laughing quietly or arguing good-naturedly.

From the voices behind him he heard the sound of a woman giggling and then heard a second female voice speaking. The presence of others hadn't been part of his plans. Bolan absorbed the information and continued on his mission.

He reached to the foot of the stairs and looked up through the opening in the ceiling. He could see a patch of dark paneled wall in the illumination from that angle but that was all.

He put his foot on the bottom rung of the staircase and began to climb. He took the next step slowly, carefully easing his weight down to avoid giving his movements away. He kept his finger poised on the trigger of the M-11.

His head approached the opening, and he reached the section where the staircase twisted on itself and he was forced to turn his back on the open hall below. He navigated that section quickly and came to the top of the spiral stairs.

Bolan did a quick double-check of the hallway below him, then craned his neck past the lip of the landing. Slowly he tracked his gaze across the room, noting open area with a table and several chairs, some low couches and a few ottomans. Potted plants had been set on either side of a large picture window now covered with a bamboo venetian blind.

Bolan saw a pair of skinny ankles peeking out between white athletic socks and the hem of dark gray trousers. The shoes were scuffed and black. The trousers ran up to a blue dress shirt. The man was busy tapping out a text message on his cell phone.

Bolan quickly cut his eyes left then right to make sure the man was alone. There appeared to be no one else in the room. Across from the man was a single door of dock wood and just on his left, were a pair of double doors made of the same material.

The man clucked to himself and began working at the keypad with renewed vigor. Bolan reached out with his left hand slowly and settled it onto the floor to steady his balance as he walked himself up the final few steps. He looked like a great cat sneaking into position for a kill.

The Ingram was leveled but held tight against his

crouched body for stability as Bolan inched forward. He settled his weight on his feet carefully as he stalked his prey. He made no noise and kept three points of contact with the ground at all times. The silenced muzzle of the Ingram never wavered.

Bolan reached the edge of the couch. He saw a P-90 submachine gun sitting next to the man on the sofa. He was close enough to smell the light scent of gun oil and see the indentation the weight of the weapon made on the furniture.

Bolan inched his right foot forward, stopped, shifted his weight and then eased his left foot up until it was even. He then leaned forward and stretched out his hand and grasped the arm of the sofa. The fabric was slick and soft under his fingers.

The man on the couch hissed suddenly and Bolan's finger tensed on the trigger of his submachine gun. The man muttered harshly under his breath and his fingers began to tap out a rapid, staccato rhythm on the cell phone keypad.

Bolan could see the beads of sweat formed like raindrops on the man's upper lip. His chin was blue with five-o'clock shadow, and a nest of wiry black hairs curled out of his ear like the legs of a spider.

The man grabbed at the collar of his shirt where it bit into the soft flesh of his neck just beneath his double chin. He lifted his chin and stretched his neck to ease his discomfort. He looked over at the double doors across the room on his right, looked down at his text message screen, then looked over to his left, toward the stairs.

Bolan's face was inches from his. The man's breath was fetid with fish and coffee.

Bolan rapped the butt of the Ingram's pistol grip hard across the man's nose, snapping the cartilage instantly. Blood squirted from the man's nostrils and his eyes clenched in pain. As he began to fall backward, Bolan grabbed him by the loose material of his shirt and jerked him up. He spun the startled man and pushed him face-first to the floor. The cell phone bounced to the ground, forgotten.

Bolan came down hard on the man's back, knee driving into his kidney. The man gurgled on his scream and the soldier shoved the muzzle of the M-11 machine pistol between the guy's lips, bruising them and chipping a tooth with his violence.

"Shut up," Bolan hissed. "Shut up or I'll kill you now."

The man's English was evidently good enough to understand death threats. He instantly grasped at his chance to live and fell silent. Bolan leaned over him putting his lips next to the man's ear.

"Just nod if you understand," he whispered.

Hesitantly, the man nodded.

"Good. Now listen. Scream and you die. Fight and you die. Try to escape and you die. Lie still and do what I tell you and you live. Do you understand?"

Slowly the man nodded. Then again, more quickly.

Bolan leaned up and pulled plastic ties from one of his web belt pouches. Moving quickly, he secured the man's hands behind his back and then bound his ankles together. Next he took out a roll of electrician tape.

As he prepped the tape, he leaned in again. "If I'd wanted to kill you, I would have. You got lucky today. Now bite on this pillow and count your blessings."

The man opened his mouth to say something but Bolan quickly jabbed him with the M-11 and he nodded instead. Bolan set the gun down and shoved one of the throw pillows off the couch into the man's face.

"Bite," he ordered. The man bit.

Quickly Bolan stretched out his tape and wound it around the man's head several times, securing the pillow in his mouth as a gag. He rose, Ingram in hand.

He dragged the man behind the couch he had just been sitting on.

The Executioner crossed the room, heading directly toward the double doors beyond the table and chair. He keyed up his com-link with Charlie Mott.

"I'm in position to finish," Bolan said, his voice low and calm. "Go ahead and bring the boat in."

Bolan lowered his hand and took up the Ingram in both hands. He eyed the door with a raider's experienced eye. It opened toward him. He ran his eyes down the door frame and determined it was not locked.

Reaching around to the back of his web belt, he pulled free the canister-shaped flash-bang grenade. He looped a finger through the pin and pulled it clear, keeping the safety level firmly in place.

Bolan reached out with the grenade in his hand and turned the doorknob. Next the grenade spoon flew off. Operating in hyper time Bolan pulled the door open and stepped back.

He swept his left arm back, then pitched the grenade forward in an underhand throw. He felt the smooth weight roll off his fingertips and leave his hand as he got his first look inside the room. Five startled faces looked up at him from a black oak conference table, their eyes wide and mouths open.

The grenade sailed into the room as Bolan lifted his leg and put his boot against the open edge of the door. He hugged the Ingram to his chest and kicked out, slamming the door closed and spinning off to the side in case someone inside the room was able to return fire.

He sank to one knee beside the door and turned his head slightly when the crack of the stun grenade went off. The doors rattled hard in their frames and the detonation hurt Bolan's ears even outside the room.

The Executioner was up and moving instantly. He opened the door and passed through it, running into the room, weapon up and ready.

He saw stunned men on the floor, sprawled across the table or slipping out of chairs. They moaned, blinded, and clamped hands to injured ears. He fired a quick burst past them across the room and blew out the picture window. He kicked one man hard in the chin as he tried to rise.

The Executioner turned and pulled the door closed behind him, then turned the dead-bolt lock into position. He spun and saw a stunned man with a beard trying to rise from the table, blood trickling from his ear. He caught the stunned man in the neck with an overhand right that felled him like a blow from a woodsman's ax.

He did a quick head count as he moved along—five men. He had expected six, but he didn't have time to complain.

Bolan snapped open a pouch on his web belt and ripped open the Velcro seals. He shoved his hand inside and came out with plastic riot cuffs. He bent and slapped a pair on the man still writhing on the floor. He stood and moved to the next one.

"Stay down or you die!" He snarled, working quickly.

He was like a circus performer entering a lion's cage. As long as he was fast and sure and agile, he could keep the men where he needed. One slip and they would be on him the same as any other caged predator.

He cuffed two more in quick succession, then saw movement from the head of the table. A terror leader he didn't recognize from intelligence photos had managed to rise and pull a handgun with a stainless-steel frame from a shoulder holster.

Bolan did not hesitate. He turned the Ingram on the man and gunned him down with a short, savage burst to the face. He saw movement at his feet and stomped a loose member of Zamira Loebis's war cabinet back to sleep, then bent and secured his cuffs.

He slid across the table to deal with the last man, the one he recognized as Zamira Loebis himself.

Bolan felt no sense of climax. He knew he wasn't out of hot water yet but that was only part of it. He felt like a blue collar factory worker at the end of one more eight-hour shift in an endless line of eight-hour shifts. He knew that when he punched out this day with Zamira Loebis, he would simply be clocking in again tomorrow.

Bolan's gratification came from running the race, not from reaching the finish line.

It was then that people began attacking the door to the room. Shoulders thudded into the wood and desperate hands tried the metal knob. There were angry shouts from outside and the familiar snaps and cracks of weapons being charged and readied. Bolan lowered the Ingram M-11 to his hip and pivoted toward the door.

He snarled and cut loose with his automatic weapon.

17

Bullets ripped through the wood of the door, ripping out gouges as the Executioner laid into structure. With grim satisfaction he heard men screaming in frantic tones at the sudden fusillade. A body the struck the door and then hit the floor, and a stream of blood poured into the room under the bottom of the entranceway.

"Stay back or I'll kill everyone in here!" Bolan shouted. "I am with the Movement of God, and your infidel brothers will be murdered if you resist this plan!"

Let them figure that one out, Bolan thought grimly.

He turned and grabbed Loebis as the man tried to rise.

"Tell them to back off or you die. Tell them about the bomb I have strapped to me," Bolan ordered.

Loebis craned his neck to try to see if he could identify the suicide vest the big American claimed he wore. Bolan jabbed the Ingram's sound suppressor at him to keep his head down.

"Just say it," Bolan said. "If you don't speak up now,

I'm going to slice the veins along the inside of your elbows and wait for you to bleed to death. After you lose about a gallon of blood, you'll wish you'd cooperated. Now do what I say."

The man began to babble out the instructions Bolan had given him, speaking so quickly he ran everything together in a frightened jumble. Bolan twisted and ripped down the ruined bamboo blind that had covered the window he'd shot out.

He looked out just as Charlie Mott guided the modified sampan into position some eighteen feet below.

The bodyguards positioned on the dock began to open up with their weapons. Mott braced himself and returned fire.

Once again the clock was ticking.

"You're not going to like this," Bolan said as he turned. Loebis looked up at him, confusion playing across his features. Bolan smiled, his eyes dark. Then the Executioner let his Ingram M-11 drop from his hands and dangled by the sling. He stepped forward and grabbed the terror leader with both hands.

"No!" Loebis shouted as Bolan pulled him onto his feet. The man struggled, but Bolan was too big and too strong. His grip never faltered as he gave the Indonesian criminal the bum's rush toward the door like a nightclub bouncer.

Loebis screamed in terror as Bolan pitched him headlong out the window. He screamed all the way down until he struck the pile of gunnysacks and the old mattress Mott had placed at the front of the sampan. The pile did little to alleviate the impact but kept the man from being smashed to death.

Loebis struck the deck and his screams became muted moans.

The Executioner put one foot on the window ledge and launched himself into space. He saw flashes of yellow flame coming off the dock as the men fired on Mott. He plunged toward the dark water of the river. He twisted in midair to clear the edge of the boat and his feet struck the water hard. Bolan plunged into the river with a splash, the black water slowing his fall. At the bottom of his drop he kicked up hard for the surface.

He broke the surface and sucked in air. Immediately he struck out in a sidestroke and reached the side of the sampan in a few quick kicks. He hauled himself up and over the side and rolled across the deck.

Bullets burned across the deck and he stayed flat on his back. He looked over and met the frightened eyes of Loebis. Bolan dropped his empty magazine out of the Ingram and reached for a new one.

"I'd stay down if I were you," he warned good-naturedly. "Your boys just might kill you."

Loebis didn't move.

Bolan seated his fresh magazine and charged a 9 mm round into the chamber. He lifted his weapon and squeezed off a long ragged burst of harassing fire toward the guards positioned at the docks.

"Let's go!" he hollered out to Mott.

"On it! Hang on!" Mott answered.

Bolan saw a flash of movement from the second-story window through which he'd made his escape. He rolled over and fired quickly. A gunman pitched out of the window and dropped like a stone, submachine gun falling from limp hands.

Bolan sprayed more bullets into the open window to provide some semblance of cover as they made their escape.

"Blow the charges!" Mott yelled.

"Negative!" Bolan shouted back as he fired another burst. "There's possible innocents inside," he said, referring to the feminine laughter he had overheard. He would take any risk to avoid killing those who weren't uninvolved.

The sampan pulled away from the house as Mott worked the outboard engines.

Bolan fired at a figure in the window, then turned and sprayed a burst at the two terrorist triggermen on the dock. Movement from the front of the house caught his attention as more gunmen from the meeting room raced out, heading toward the boats tied up to the docks.

The Executioner fired a third burst in their direction as Mott wheeled the front of the sampan around and pushed the boat toward the open water. Bolan rose to one knee and triggered a tight burst at the second-story window and saw his rounds pock the wall to the left of the opening. Mott finished turning the boat and Bolan heard the engines drop as they began to churn water at a serious rate, forcing the sampan to pick up speed.

Mott was running for open water and the rendezvous coordinates, but he was forced to slalom in and out of the congested river traffic. Several times Bolan tensed his finger on the curve of his trigger only to abort his shot rather than risk putting rounds to near the vessels of innocent bystanders.

The terrorists were not so restrained.

Gunmen crowded the bows of their two pursuing speedboats and fired with indiscriminate aggression at the fleeing sampan. The reports of their weapons were sharp but muted in competition with the roars of the powerful engines propelling the racing craft. Their muzzle-flashes were bright star patterns that burst out of the darkness. Bullets cut through the air between the crouched Mott and Bolan, and geysers erupted in linear patterns in the water around them.

The speedboats cut and darted between the multitude of craft tethered in the river more agile than the speedy converted sampan Mott navigated. The speedboats began to cut the distance between the craft in leaps and bounds.

Bullets struck the wooden hull of the sampan with greater frequency. A sudden line of slugs tore gouges out of the wooden hull, spinning splinters into the air like grenade shrapnel. Bolan ducked his face away instinctively.

He popped his head back up and fired. He saw his own rounds strike the hull of the closest boat, leaving dark holes along the flared structure of the vessel. The men beside the boat driver returned his fire but Bolan had found his range.

His next burst shattered part of the windshield. Glass sprayed up into one gunman's face and he dropped his weapon and spun away, his hands flying up to his injured face. The speedboat's racing momentum was a deadly trap in its own right. The man's hip struck the edge of the boat and he was overbalanced.

He fell out of the craft and hit the water hard, making a sharp flat splash as the river sucked him under.

The man's teammates did not try to rescue him but continued to press the pursuit. The only gunman left in the boat tried another burst. This time he was more accurate and his bullets sliced through the air between Mott and Bolan and struck the deck near Loebis.

The powerboat pulled closer as the two vessels were forced to suddenly circle the inert bulk of a garbage scow and then quickly cut away from an anchored fishing boat.

Bolan saw his opportunity. He grabbed Mott's Kalashnikov carbine and squeezed the trigger with smooth skill.

The 5.45 mm bullet burned out on a flat trajectory and struck the speedboat on the left, one inch above the feathered spray of river water in the aft compartment of the watercraft.

The powerboat went up like a Roman candle. A ball of orange fire and jet black smoke engulfed the craft in a sizzling flash, and bodies were sent spinning like pinwheels as the vessel leaped straight into the air and turned over in a broken somersault.

Flaming pieces of the craft began to strike the black water, casting weird reflections as they were extinguished. The speedboat sank quickly and dark smoke, blacker than the night, formed like fog above the slow moving water.

Bolan winced back from the light and the sound of the detonation then turned his weapon toward the second speedboat. He saw the vessel suddenly perform a tight 180-degree turn and run in the opposite direction.

Grimly satisfied Bolan lowered the Kalashnikov.

He turned toward Mott as he set the weapon aside. Behind them the burning wreckage and spilled fuel continued to burn on the river. Brunei emergency services vehicles would soon be on the scene, and the Stony Man operatives needed to be far away by then.

"I'll call Jack," Bolan said, "and arrange the pickup."

Mott nodded. He put the sampan in the center of the river where the current was strongest and pushed through the night.

ZAMIRA LOEBIS WAS NOT an ideologue. He was neither a political extremist nor a religious zealot. He was man motivated by the twin gods of wealth and power, and when it came to brutal interrogation he had no inner wells of strength to draw upon.

He babbled like a baby in the hands of the Executioner, and Bolan extracted the information he needed to end his Indonesian operation. From the lips of the mercenary terror merchant Bolan was able to extract the names of corrupt government officials Washington could go after, including the men who were responsible for the murdered State Department agent.

He knew it was only a small dent in the armor of evil that covered the region, but it was a start.

ROOM 59

THERE'S A FINE LINE BETWEEN DOING YOUR JOB—AND DOING THE RIGHT THING

After a snatch-and-grab mission on a quiet London street turns sour, new Room 59 operative David Southerland is branded a cowboy. While his quick thinking gained valuable intelligence, breaching procedure is a fatal mistake that can end a career—or a life. With his future on the line, he's tasked with a high-speed chase across London to locate a sexy thief with stolen global-security secrets that have more than one interested—and very dangerous—player in the game....

Look for

THE finish line

by

cliff RYDER

ROGUE ANGEL™

SWORDSMAN'S LEGACY
by AleX Archer

For Annja Creed, finding a Musketeer's sword is a dream come true. Until it becomes a nightmare.

In need of a break from work, archaeologist Annja Creed visits France to indulge one of her greatest fantasies: finding D'Artagnan's lost sword. The rapier has been missing since the seventeenth century, and Ascher Vallois, one of Annja's treasure-hunting friends, believes he has located the site of the relic. But Annja learns Vallois has made a huge sacrifice to protect the sword and its secret from a relic hunter. And the man won't stop until he gets everything he wants—including Annja.

Available November wherever books are sold.

GRA15

JAMES AXLER

DEATH LANDS

Plague Lords

In a ruined world, past and future clash with terrifying force...

The sulfur-teeming Gulf of Mexico is the poisoned end of earth, but here, Ryan and the others glean rumors of whole cities deep in South America that survived the blast intact. But as the companions contemplate a course of action, a new horror approaches on the horizon. The Lords of Death are Mexican pirates raiding stockpiles with a grim vengeance. When civilization hits rock bottom, a new stone age will emerge, with its own personal day of blood reckoning.

In the Deathlands, the future could always be worse. Now it is...

Available December wherever you buy books.

GEIBC